Alan Hunter

Death on the Heath

Walker and Company
New York

Also by Alan Hunter:
The Honfleur Decision
The Scottish Decision

First published in the United States of America in
1982 by the Walker Publishing Company, Inc.

ISBN: 0-8027-5468-8

Library of Congress Catalog Card Number: 81-71199

Printed in the United States of America

10 9 8 7 6 5 4 3 2 1

1

Gently awoke with a start to find sun outlining the curtains of the big bedroom and to hear, outside in Lime Walk, the cheery clatter of milk delivery. For some moments he lay quite still; then he reached out and felt beside him. But all his hand met was cold sheets and, turning, he saw the undinted pillow.

It was a huge room, much too large, and just then almost devoid of furniture: you got the impression of camping out or of a temporary billet in wartime. Across the hall was another huge room containing only two fireside chairs. Then, at the back, there was an empty kitchen and a bathroom with a single towel.

Outside the milk-trolley whirred and passed on, while someone was trying to start a car. One heard distant traffic; shadows of leaves stirred on the sun-flooded curtains. And he was alone there, quite alone, hugging a corner of this anonymous nowhere, in a part of London he scarcely knew: a flat that smelt vaguely of furniture warehouses.

Grunting, he felt on the floor for his pipe: as yet they hadn't got round to buying bedside tables! All the same they'd been lucky to get that flat, the lease of which had been handed on by a retiring colleague. Lucky to get it: but could he ever settle there, in those rooms the size of station booking-halls? Alone, he felt like a bit of left luggage, some human flotsam that had lost its label.

He grunted again, shoved his feet into cold shoes and hiked across the hall for his paper. Three days they had been in the flat, returning to it straight from the honeymoon. Perhaps at first the glamour had spilled over to the flat, which he'd seen only in terms of its convenience – between Kensington Church Street and Holland Park, ideal both for him and for Gabrielle. For him five stations on the Circle Line, for her easy access to Heathrow. The emptiness, the vast rooms and warehouse-smell ... why hadn't he noticed them till now?

Grumpily he shuffled into the kitchen and filled the kettle for his pot of tea. In the sink lay the dirty coffee things of the previous evening, coffee he had drunk while waiting for her call. The parting had been traumatic: so soon afterwards! In the departure lounge they had both been brave. Then, when her flight was called, her smile had scarcely lasted till she'd turned to leave, running...

Yet they had known this would be routine, that business would regularly call her back to France. Perhaps ... after this first time? Even last night, the flat had remained steeped in her presence.

He placed a bowl of wheatflakes on the teatray and shambled back with it to the bedroom, where in fact a windowseat was the only place to set it down. The sun, when he pulled the tall curtains, burst into the room almost indecently; across the road, a woman getting in her milk paused to stare at his pyjama-clad figure.

What was he doing here? Up in Finchley Mrs Jarvis, his housekeeper, would also be stirring; would by now, had he returned there, be knocking on his door with a breakfast-tray. And then the familiar routine would follow, as it had done for so many years, in his own house, among his own things, with neighbours who smiled when they caught his eye! Had it all ended, and so completely? He had taken Gabrielle to Finchley, she avid with curiosity to see the home of the man who had swept her into church ... And suddenly, for him too, it had become a strange place, stamped with another man's personality. How could it have happened? Even Mrs Jarvis had treated him with reserve, almost with resentment.

'My friend,' Gabrielle had said when they left, 'that woman is wondering if there is still a place for her in your household.'

And it was so. With shock he had realised that he could never return to live in Elphinstone Road. The man who had lived there was no longer himself: himself had been pitchforked into the street. Then live where? In this drum of a flat? But that was a convenience, not a home! They had discussed it but come to no decision except that both wanted a home outside London. ...

He ate his wheatflakes sombrely, sitting there in the window-seat, staring now and then at the paper, which he'd propped against the sill. This was a low spot, that was all: Monday morning and Gabrielle gone. No need to panic ... Soon she would be back, and they'd go out to buy furniture for those empty rooms.

He bathed, shaved, dressed and went to the mews to collect his car. The sunny morning, which made the streets quite gay, did nothing to improve his grouchy mood. All the weekend had been rainy: today they chose to restart summer! Typists, office-workers hurrying to work were wearing light clothes, as though off to a beach.

It was no better at the Yard, where file-carrying colleagues came up to slap him on the shoulder, or to tell him about the collection which his whirlwind wedding had made retrospective. In his office, bleak with inoccupancy, he found cards and a giant bouquet. The latter, composed of chrysanthemums, made the place smell like a funeral parlour.

'How did it go, Chief?'

That was Dutt, who had been hovering at the communicating door. Behind him was Blondie, the AC's nubile secretary, who no doubt had been responsible for the flowers. Everyone smiling ...

Did they take him for the same man who had walked out of that office just three weeks before?

'Sir, the AC would like to see you right away,' Blondie said. 'I think it's about something that came in from Suffolk.'

That put the tin hat on it. If he were out in the country, Gabrielle would be ringing an empty flat.

'So what's happened in Suffolk?'

'It's a stabbing case, sir, the managing director of a firm of printers. Only they think his wife was involved, also a boy friend called Reymerston.'

'Reymerston ...!'

His stare must have been forbidding, because Blondie's azure gaze faltered.

'Where did it happen?'

'Near Wolmering, sir. But I forget the name of the village.'

'Reymerston,' Dutt repeated thoughtfully. 'Chief, wasn't that the chummie who confessed to the Selly job?'

In the Assistant Commissioner (Crime)'s office sun was laying bars on the bouncy carpet, and the AC was engaged in the devotional coffee-making which, with him, had replaced an addiction to cigarettes. Beside a percolator beginning to bubble stood two tiny, fragile cups, a screw-lid silver canister and a small silver bowl of

Demerara sugar. Cream there was not: the AC regarded cream as a taste for peasants.

'Ah ... our matrimonial casualty. Take a pew while I pour, Gently.'

Gently sat. Pushed aside on the desk were a couple of files, both open.

'How was France?'

Gently merely shrugged. Did one answer such questions? 'We came back on Wednesday.'

'Ah yes, Wednesday. Gave yourself time to settle in.'

As though it came at ten guineas a bottle the AC was decanting his jet-black brew. As time passed it had got stronger and stronger till you could smell it being distilled when you stepped from the lift.

'Here.'

Gently took his cup, but contented himself with inhaling. With thin, pursed lips the AC sipped an experimental mouthful.

'Now. It's providential your coming back on the strength this morning, Gently. Something has come in right up your alley – in fact, you've been specially asked for.' He pulled up a file and settled his glasses. 'No doubt you'll remember Andrew Reymerston?'

'I remember him.'

'Ye-es,' the AC said. 'Not one of your most scintillating cases, was he? According to your report he confessed to killing the Selly woman, not to mention a large-scale embezzlement. Yet the case is still on the file.'

'It was an unsupported confession.'

'But *you* believed him?'

'He made the confession to me in private. He refused to repeat it before witnesses and there wasn't a scrap of evidence to connect him.'

'But you believed him – yes or no?'

Unwillingly Gently nodded. 'We had an open-and-shut case against another man but had to drop it after Reymerston's confession. It showed sufficient cognisance of the crime to make it unsafe to proceed.'

He took a sip of the AC's corrosive brew. Here was a fine business to come back to! Reymerston: an ache lying in his past, a man he had always tried to forget. They'd had another man – a

4

Major Rede – in a double bind because his niece had been deeply implicated: had only to break him, and he was tottering. And then Reymerston had thrown his spanner.

Yes, a failure ... and a bitter one. The more so because he had damaged an innocent man.

'A pity,' the AC was saying. 'But not to worry, you're getting a second bite at the cherry. There's been another job near Wolmering and Reymerston is the man the locals fancy.' He pulled over the other file. 'Perhaps you've heard of the Tallis Press?'

'The which ...?'

'Please pay attention, Gently! Getting married doesn't seem to have sharpened your wits.' The AC stared waspishly for an instant before returning to his file. 'They're a firm of printers and book manufacturers with works at Stansgate, twelve miles from Wolmering, and the managing director, Frederick Quennell, lived at Walderness, across the river from Wolmering. You know of it?'

'I've seen it.'

'Then perhaps you'll know there's a yacht club there. On Saturday Quennell seems to have rung the yacht club to say he'd be missing the first race. He didn't turn up for the second either, and yesterday morning they found the body. It was on a heath outside the village. He had been stabbed in the back.'

Gently said nothing. The AC sipped and turned a sheet in the file.

'Ah yes – here we have it. They found a letter on the body. An anonymous letter in a feminine hand, making a rendezvous at the place where they found him. The locals went through his papers looking for a match for the handwriting, then they showed it to the family, and that put the cat among the pigeons. It was his wife's writing. She denied it and swore the letter was a forgery. The son shut up tight and the daughter had some sort of fit. The wife then volunteered an alibi of visiting a friend, only she forgot to warn the friend, who was in London at the time. Promising, eh?'

Gently hunched. 'Weren't there dabs on the letter?'

The AC frowned, skimming a sheet. 'Nothing down here, but I dare say the paper was soggy because of Saturday night's rain. Anyway, the locals snouted around some more and came up with a fistful of gossip. Frederick Quennell was estranged from his wife and had a long-running affair with a secretary. Meanwhile his wife was a model of rectitude – or that's what everybody thought; only she wasn't. When her alibi was bust she had to come out with a better story.'

'Reymerston?'

'Exactly. She spent the afternoon with him in a friend's cottage. And the cottage is only a mile away from the spot where Quennell's body was found. He's a painter, is he?'

Gently nodded.

'Said he was painting a great way off. But then La Quennell must have got in touch with him, because he changed his story to square with hers.'

'Any confirmation?'

'None mentioned ... Of course, the locals turned him over. They took a steel letter-opener from his house that might have been the weapon, but apparently wasn't. What the lab specifies is something similar, but of circular section ... poetical references to poniards and stilettos. Quennell was killed by a single blow.' The AC sat back. 'So that's it. The locals have come to a stand. The wife continues to swear that the letter is a forgery, she and Reymerston back each other's alibis, the son's alibi is provable and the daughter's memory refuses to return. A nice one, as they say. With the locals understandably backing Reymerston.'

Gently ventured another sip. 'They think it may have been a deliberate plot?'

The AC stared sapiently. 'Either way would fit the bill, I imagine. Quennell could have happened on the letter by chance, or had it shoved under his nose. Is Reymerston a devious type?'

'He's certainly clever.'

'Getting away with it last time may have made him cheeky.'

'At the same time, it wasn't very clever to leave the letter on the corpse.'

The AC removed and dandled his glasses. 'Well – that's for you to sort out, Gently. And this time there is some evidence, so I'm anticipating a result.' He closed the file and pushed it across. 'You know the local man, Inspector Eyke. Give him a ring before you leave – and remember to give my love to Suffolk.'

Back in his office, someone, Blondie, had found a jug for the flowers, while on the desk lay an absurd caricature depicting himself, pipe in mouth, a chain dragging from his ankle.

Recognisably the work of Pagram, it was captioned: 'Benedick, the Married Man'.

He rang Eyke, who wasn't in, thought of ringing Rouen, but didn't. By now Gabrielle would be out at the china factory, choosing new stock from their showrooms ...

And meanwhile, at Lime Walk, was a desolate flat, and up in Finchley an alien house. And now Reymerston: again.

He picked up his away-bag and went down to the car.

Sun followed him up the A12. When he drove into Wolmering the small town was drowsing in midday heat, its narrow main street thronged with visitors in spite of its being early September. Coming along, he had stopped in a lay-by to remove his jacket and roll up his sleeves; yet the heat was not oppressive, just the kindly warmth of late summer. He had passed by fields of burning stubble, the smoke lazy in still air, and once a purple rash of heather; then there'd been verges yellow with ragwort.

At the police-station Eyke must have been watching out for him, since he appeared at once when Gently parked. He shook hands shyly; five years had altered little in his anxious, wry-nosed face.

Unlike Gently he was neatly dressed and even sported a discreet tie. He hesitated awkwardly before plucking up courage to say: 'I'm told you're just back from your honeymoon, sir ...'

Gently grunted and followed him into his office. Nothing had changed much there, either. Looking round, Gently recognised the very chair where the Major had sat when they were demolishing him ... five years since: while, in hospital, his niece was having aspirin pumped from her stomach.

And Reymerston, had he gone on living here, knowing that the police knew what they knew ...?

He growled: 'What happened to the Major?'

Deferentially, Eyke had ushered him to the chair at the desk: he himself had taken a chair in front of it, where he sat embarrassedly, like a visitor.

'Cleared out, sir. He went down south ... Budleigh Salterton, I think it was. He went to stay in Felixstowe for a time, till they found a buyer for the house.'

'And the niece?'

'Went back to Jamaica. Her father was vice-consul there.'

'And Selly?'

'Don't know about him, sir.' After a pause, Eyke added: 'He was at the funeral.'

Yes, that checked: for all his brash callousness, Selly'd had some feeling for his abandoned wife. Not very much, not nearly enough: about what you would accord to an unloved dog. He had married her, he said, because she wasn't like the others, because he'd never known what made her tick. That was her tragedy: nothing had made her tick. She'd just gone on trying, until ...

'So what's your opinion of Reymerston now?'

Eyke's eyes had taken on a cautious expression. About his opinion at the time Gently'd had no doubt: it was that Reymerston's confession had been a clever trick. Eyke hadn't wanted the demoralising job of bringing the Major to his knees; he'd jumped at the confession. For him, it was enough that Gently had believed it.

'Sir, we did send a copy of your report to Birmingham.'

Because there had lain the hook-up with Vivienne Selly. Under his former name of Reginald Aston, Reymerston had been chief accountant of a firm of manufacturing chemists. Aplan, Rayner Ltd had made a bomb from the reckless marketing of untested drugs, then they'd gone bust, and the Fraud Squad was called to investigate a deficit of half a million. The evidence had pointed to Joseph Rayner and a clique of his associates: nobody apparently had given a thought to Reymerston, who had resigned his position a few months earlier. His wife had died: natural enough for a grief-stricken man to drop out of sight ...

'Did nothing come of it?'

'They went through the motions, sir. I had a talk on the phone with one of the Squad. He as much as said jolly good luck to anybody who could put one over on Joe Rayner. But I don't think they believed it, sir. They seemed quite certain about who had the money.'

'Andrew Reymerston is Reginald Aston and Vivienne Selly worked in his department.'

'Yes, sir, but what threat was she to him, when all she knew was he'd changed his name?'

'She could have tried it on.'

'He'd have laughed in her face, sir. And she was into the Major's ribs already.'

'The Major resisted and she backed down.'

'Sir, we've only the Major's word for that.'

But Vivienne Selly had tried it on; so Reymerston had told him, and it fitted. At the end of the line, without hope, she had made her last, forlorn play. In the dark night she had gone to his cottage and made a pass at shaking him down; and he, like the Major, had said no; and Vivienne had always taken no for an answer. But she didn't leave the cottage. According to Reymerston, a little later he heard her call him from upstairs. There he'd found her lying naked on the bed, and staring at him with her strange eyes. Something had clicked in him. There was in the bedroom a plastic wrapper from a new mattress; he had taken it and wrapped it round her, then placed a pillow over her face. She hadn't resisted; by his own account she had somehow willed him to do it. But when, a few seconds later, he'd removed the pillow, Vivienne Selly had treacherously died.

Avowedly the confession was made to save the Major, and there hadn't been a cobweb of proof; but it fitted; and it explained how she'd died, which had baffled both Gently and the forensic laboratory. The corpse, when they found it, had been immaculate, the face in an expression of profound peace.

Gently said plangently: 'Yet you're gunning for him now, and apparently on the flimsiest of evidence.'

'Sir, he gave a false alibi ...'

'And what would you expect, if he was on a date with a married woman? Did you tell him what it was about?'

'Well ... no, sir.'

'So he was trying to protect this Mrs Quennell. And all you got from frisking his place was a possible weapon that didn't do it ...'

It was too absurd. He was seeking to defend Reymerston, whom he believed to be a killer; whereas Eyke, who had never believed it, was seeking to hang a killing on him. Why was he taking such a stupid line ... as though, in some odd way, he owed Reymerston something?

'Let me see that letter.'

Eyke was thoroughly rattled; he stumbled clumsily in going to fetch the file. He must have been thinking, like the AC, that marriage had scarcely improved Gently.

'Here, sir. And a sample of her writing.'

The letter was little more than a note. Written on white

9

Basildon Bond notepaper, it was blurred and stained by rain. It was headed simply: 'Saturday Morning' and continued:

Dear Man,

I know you want to see me, and I want to see you too. During the racing this afternoon I shall be waiting at Gorse Circle. You know the place? I can be there at 2.30, and it's always deserted on a Saturday. Don't disappoint me, and I won't disappoint you!!! I'm tired of being a
'Neglected Woman'

The envelope, which matched, bore no address; it had been torn open roughly. The sample of Mrs Quennell's writing was a copy of a recipe for saffron cake.

'Have you had this vetted by an expert ...?'

The blurring by rain was unfortunate. It probably meant that no positive opinion was possible one way or the other. But at sight there seemed no reason to doubt the common identity of the two hands.

'How would she have sent this to Reymerston?'

'Well, sir, I'm guessing the daughter. She went off the deep end when she saw it, and nobody's got sense out of her since.'

'Wouldn't a phone call have been less risky?'

Reymerston, it appeared, no longer lived in Wolmering. Like the Major, he had sold up and moved, though in his case merely across the river. His house in Hare Lane, Walderness, was only a short distance from the Quennells'.

'Any problems at the business?'

Eyke shook his head: Tallis Press was a thriving concern. A long-established firm, it was in the process of re-equipping with electronic typesetting. One got an impression of Quennell as a buzzing executive directing his firm with a confident touch, a man who worked hard and played hard: he raced his Dragon yacht every weekend. His secretary and mistress, Marilyn Lawrence, was a yachtswoman and shared in his sport.

'What's her form?'

'County family, sir. She's very cut up by what's happened. She was waiting for him at the yacht club. She lives in an executive flat in Stansgate.'

'Where was the daughter that afternoon?'

10

'Here in Wolmering, sir. She'd come in shopping with Mrs Tallis, who's the wife of another director.'

'Living in Walderness?'

'Yes, sir. At Caxton Lodge, by the river. Her husband is Raymond Tallis, whose grandfather founded the Press.'

Gently stared a moment. 'Are they the only connections of the firm resident in the village?'

'Well, there's the son,' Eyke said. 'Young Frank Quennell. He was his father's assistant.'

'What's his story?'

'We checked him out, sir. He was in Stansgate with his fiancée. He went in before lunch, and called later at the works to pick up some estimates.'

Innocence everywhere: when it came to the crunch, you had to keep looking straight at Reymerston. Just one small point that needed explaining to keep the picture bright and clear.

'If Quennell intercepted this letter, how would Reymerston know he had a rendezvous to keep?'

'There's only one answer to that, sir,' Eyke said promptly. 'It was a put-up job to get Quennell out there.'

'Involving the daughter?'

'I don't see why not, sir. They could have gambled on her blowing the gaff to her father.'

'Also on her subsequent loss of memory?'

Eyke looked down his wry nose.

'I see it this way, sir. They never expected that letter to be found. Reymerston should have taken it off the body, then we would never have had a smell. Only he didn't, so they were caught short and had to patch up a tale.'

Gently stared. 'And you're happy with that?'

'Yes, sir. I think so.' But he didn't sound happy.

'Come on,' Gently said, rising. 'Let's get out there and look it over.'

A foot-ferry crossed the river to Walderness, but by road it was nine miles: a detour to a bridge on the A12 watched over by a lofted church. Here the river spread out in mudflats which the tide was beginning to flood, an expanse fledged with reed and notched by black, rotting piles. They turned seaward again; umbrella-headed pines made dark shapes against the water; then the narrow road was wandering through heath and obscurely pointing towards a square flint tower.

'Here, sir.'

There was no division between the heath and the road. Gently drove off on to grass and bracken where other cars had parked before him. At this point the heath was a maze of gorse, green now without flower, through which, however, one could still glimpse the river over open heath below. Eyke pointed to the gorse.

'He shoved his car in there, sir. One of my men spotted tracks leaving the road.'

'Is this the only road to the village?'

'Yes, sir.'

'So then Quennell's son would have come this way.'

'Well ... yes, sir.'

'And the daughter with Mrs Tallis.'

Eyke stared but said nothing.

They got out to examine the spot, innocent and fragrant in the lazy sun. Half a mile off the church tower peered above a fan of trees. Paths went among the bracken and heather beyond the gorse, but they were deserted. Down across the river, chalk white, Wolmering's lighthouse jutted over the town roofs.

'He left his house when?'

'Just before two, sir. He would have driven straight out here. He was dressed in sailing gear, ready to go down to his yacht.'

'E.T.D.?'

'Between two and three.'

His just having eaten lunch was a bonus for forensic.

'Carry on.'

Eyke led the way through the alleys of green gorse. At some hundred yards' distance they came to an area where the gorse formed an extensive thicket. Not far from the road, it presented an appearance of complete impregnability; nevertheless a way was clear for a car to have driven up to it.

'This way, sir.'

Eyke led him round it; and then suddenly one saw that the thicket was hollow. Stepping through a gap, one entered an amphitheatre of about thirty yards diameter. Still, scented with the green gorse, floored with short, rabbit-bitten turf, it had almost the appearance of design, of being some relic of prehistory.

'He was lying just there, sir.'

In the file had been photographs that showed the body a few steps from the gap. Quennell had been stabbed, it appeared, when entering, to finish up face down, head towards the centre. He had been killed by the one violent blow of an assailant who had come from behind.

'Now look at this, sir.'

Eyke vanished suddenly into the gorse adjacent to the gap. Gently followed; they entered a tiny chamber in the heart of the bushes.

'Look ...'

A branch had been freshly cut, permitting a view of the amphitheatre: one stared through it at precisely the spot where Quennell's body had lain.

'Would you say it wasn't premeditated now, sir?'

'Are you suggesting that the murderer made that peep-hole?'

'I'm damned certain of it, sir! This is where he stood, watching for Quennell to come by.'

'And then went out and stabbed him?'

'What else, sir?'

'Coming out of this gorse without a sound?'

'Well ... you wouldn't make much, sir.'

'Go and stand where he stood and listen for me coming out behind you.'

Eyke hesitated, then pushed his way out. Watching intently, Gently saw Eyke's head and shoulders pass by the aperture. Then he too emerged, taking every care to tread silently and hold back the gorse; but the effort was vain. In the sunny stillness his every motion was signalled.

'So?'

'Well, I don't know, sir ...' Eyke still looked unconvinced. 'Chummie had to hide somewhere, and that's the only place close to the circle.'

'Suppose he wasn't hiding, but came with Quennell.'

Eyke stared a second, then shook his head. 'No, sir, I'm not buying that. Quennell wouldn't want company when he was spying on his missus.'

'Then suppose it was he who was hiding ...'

Gently broke off, his hand on Eyke's arm. A girl had appeared from among the gorse bushes and was gazing at them with wide, dark eyes. She was young, in her teens, with a sturdy but shapely figure, her smooth, pale face bracketed by dark hair caught up behind. She stood quite still, quite expressionless, not more than twenty yards from them.

'It's the daughter ...' Eyke muttered.

'What's her name?'

'Miss Fiona.'

Smiling, Gently called: 'Miss Fiona! Were you looking for us?'

Still she simply stood gazing, without a flicker in the brown eyes. As though she were in a different world, seeing people whose voices she couldn't hear.

'Miss Fiona ...?'

Gently took a step forward, when immediately she turned and darted away. Walking slowly after her, he saw her snatch up a bicycle, run it to the road and pedal off towards the village.

'The little devil!' Eyke exclaimed, coming up behind. 'Get her to talk, and we'd know everything. But we can catch her at the house.'

Gently didn't reply.

'She was listening to us,' Eyke said.

2

'Have forensic any fresh ideas about the weapon?'

They had returned to the sun-warmed car; Gently was sitting half-in, half-out of it, letting heat leak from the muggy interior.

The trouble was that he was still feeling only casually involved in this affair of the East Anglian printer, notwithstanding the complication of Reymerston ... or was it perhaps just because of that complication?

For example, seeing the Quennell girl pedal away, he had been switched back immediately to Gabrielle – something about the girl's stocky figure must have done it, because otherwise she bore no resemblance. In a flash he was seeing Gabrielle long since, when she had been a teenager too: speeding off on a bicycle, just like that, on some girlish ramble by Dives or Houlgate. A Gabrielle he could never know caught suddenly in the flying figure: which, to Eyke, had been merely part of the case, a wilful obstruction; an irritant. Was this how it was when one got married – to be swept back continually into private worlds? For a moment his business there seemed curiously irrelevant, as though he had caught a glimpse from a transcending viewpoint ...

'They think it may have been a one-off, sir, a job that chummie faked up. A bit of steel rod with a point. Either that or an old-fashioned dagger.'

'A bit of steel rod ...'

'It was round-sectioned, sir. You don't see many jobs like that. I asked them if it could have been a bayonet, but they wouldn't say yes or no.'

'How well have you searched the area?'

'We had dogs and men with metal-detectors.'

'Has Reymerston tools?'

'There's a vice in his garage, and an old hacksaw with a broken blade.'

But you couldn't really see Reymerston in his garage, solemnly fashioning a weapon for murder: sawing off a length of rod and filing away at it, clamped in the vice. A wrong picture ...

'Get on to forensic and press them for something more definite.'

'Yes, sir. But if chummie did make the weapon, not much doubt then about premeditation.'

He surprised Eyke in a quizzical look: not at all the Gently he remembered, the look said! Well, perhaps it wasn't. Sitting beside Eyke was a man whose home had suddenly become nowhere ...

'Do we get after the Quennell girl, sir?'

With an effort, Gently hauled his feet into the car. While they had been parked there, a matter of twenty minutes, only half-a-dozen vehicles had passed. On Saturday afternoon, would there have been more? With perhaps ramblers on the paths that crossed the heath? But the writer of the letter at least had been confident that the spot was secure from observation ...

He slammed his door. 'Where's Reymerston's place?'

'Sir, if we caught up with the girl now ...'

Gently shook his head: not a chance. He had to see Reymerston, face to face.

They drove past a sign and outlying houses and the massy but ruinous church; then they were descending a slightly crooked street bordered by period houses and cottages. In brick or plaster, with roofs ·of pantile, they crowded close to the narrow thoroughfare, some pressing quite up to it with little bays and mullioned windows. A stores was set back at a junction; an antique shop, a post office blended with the houses; further down one saw an old-fashioned garage, and beyond it a comfortable-looking inn. The village breathed modest affluence: houses, cottages were well kept. Finally the street bore left towards the river, while ahead, between marram hills, lay a panel of sea.

'No poverty here ...'

'No, sir. Property fetches a price in Walderness.'

Many of the loiterers they were having to slow for were elderly people, stylishly dressed. A village with tone: at the end of its one road, with a foot-ferry across to town, the river and yacht club at its door and, over the sandhills, beach and sea. Quennell had been no fool when he settled here, twelve miles from the racket of the presses in Stansgate. If Wolmering were sweet, this was sweeter:

sea and Suffolk and county rates ...

'What sort of car had Quennell?'

'A Rolls, sir.'

Of course. In which he would have left late and returned early.

Eyke indicated an anonymous junction and they turned off into a leafy by-road. Behind trees one could see intriguing houses nursed by shrubs and set in spacious gardens. Then, at a bend, came a surprise prospect across hayfields, marsh and river: Wolmering, clustered along its ridge and cutting off sharply into a haze of sea.

'Which house?'

'Next on the right, sir.'

Like Reymerston's previous dwelling, this one was modest: a white-plastered cottage, tucked up high, with a big picture window turned to the view. Trees backed it, and a steep drive led to parking at the side; a timber garage had open doors that revealed a metallic blue Renault 4L.

Gently drove in and parked. There was movement behind the big window. Moments later a man appeared at the door; he was wearing a stained smock and held a brush in his hand.

'You let nothing hinder your work, I see!'

'My dear old lad, what would you expect?'

It happened instantly with this man: you had to fight down an automatic instinct to accept him. The shy eyes, smiling mouth, strong features, active bearing: along with them went a sort of self-mocking gaiety almost impossible to resist.

'That's exactly what I would expect. In these things you look for a pattern.'

'So, I'm a painter.'

'What bothers me is where you go for your inspiration.'

Reymerston ducked his head, grinning. 'Come in, old lad, and get it off your chest! As a matter of fact I was knocking off for lunch. I suppose I can't offer you two a bite?'

'No, you can't.'

'It was only cheese, anyway. I'll ring The Gull and book you a table.'

Gently was beginning to feel ridiculous, like a child who'd got stuck with a fit of sulks. He had worked up a level of indignation that plainly he wasn't going to be allowed to maintain. Yet he didn't mean to be charmed out of it either! He made his face into a blank. Only by keeping Reymerston at arm's length could one hope to deal with the fellow ...

They followed him into a hall, on the walls of which hung water-colours. Gently recognised a Miles Edmund Cotman that had hung in the cottage across the river. Then into a studio-lounge surprisingly similar to the one he had known before, with the remembered picture-racks, furniture, books and pervading smell of linseed oil. On an easel stood a canvas, just begun, a palette gory with colours lying near it. In some corner of his mind, Gently registered that Reymerston had changed his style and was no longer a pointillist. The painter dabbled his brush, then wiped it.

'Sit yourselves while I make that call.'

When he returned he'd got rid of the smock to reveal himself in a cerise shirt.

'Now ... a beer?'

Gently merely stared at him. Reymerston smiled and squatted on a stool. The thing was getting more and more absurd – with Reymerston grinning, as though coaxing him to begin!

'Let's get one thing straight to start with. Your alibi isn't worth two pins.'

'Granted,' Reymerston smiled. 'I've had a go at it myself, trying to fill in the gaps.'

'This is a serious matter!'

'Oh, quite. But you do see the difficulty we're in. The essence of a rendezvous is discretion, and discreet is what we were being on Saturday. Have you seen Archie's cottage?'

Gently grunted.

'Well, it's very much on its own. And you can shove two cars in behind it so they're out of sight from the road. It's down Platten's Loke, which goes nowhere and ends in a track over heath. Only a few bird-watchers and horse-riders use it, and I'm damned if I can find a witness.'

'What time do you say you got there?'

'At two. Ruth came a little later.'

'How much later?'

'Oh ... ten minutes. I'd only just unlocked and opened some windows.'

'So where was the owner?'

'Archie Todd has a studio in Chelsea. He comes down here for odd weekends – I keep an eye on the place for him.'

'How convenient for you.'

Reymerston didn't smile. 'Ruth isn't just a pick-up, you know.' He looked straight at Gently. 'Have you spoken to her yet?'

Gently didn't reply.

'She's a very fine person who's had a rotten deal in her marriage. Quennell was a pig of a man – a success-merchant, quite unscrupulous. He reminded me of Joe Rayner. But at least Joe treated his wife decently.'

'Quennell wasn't worthy of her, you'd say.'

Reymerston said softly: 'I want to marry her.'

'And now you can.'

Just as softly, Reymerston said: 'Yes – if she'll have me.'

'And isn't that the nub of it?'

Their eyes held. Suddenly, Reymerston jumped up and took steps down the room. He turned, looked towards Eyke, then back again to Gently.

'I want to talk to you alone.'

'Oh no,' Gently said emphatically. 'There'll be none of that this time. Anything you want to confess you'll confess with the Inspector present.'

'This isn't a confession.'

'Then the Inspector can stay.'

'What I have to say is for your ears only.'

'You can talk quite freely.'

'That's just what I can't do. And you need to hear what I can tell you.'

It was close to blackmail. Reymerston's mouth was set in an obstinate line. And he was right: there was that between them which couldn't be broached in front of Eyke, whose ears had cocked already at the casual reference to Joseph Rayner.

Shrugging profoundly, Gently nodded to Eyke. 'Perhaps you can wait in the car.'

'If you think it's wise, sir.'

After a pregnant pause, Eyke rose and strode from the studio. They saw him pass the window, heard the clap of the car door. Reymerston came back up the room.

'I could see he was cramping your style,' he smiled. 'So now what about a beer?'

Gently took out his pipe. What was the use?

'Make mine a bitter.'

The beer came in bottles bearing the label of the family brewery of which Wolmering boasted. When he had poured it and taken a long swallow, Reymerston fixed Gently with an amused eye.

'You're married, they tell me.'

'Never mind that!'

'It may help you to understand my position better. Off the cuff, would you murder the husband of a woman you wanted to marry?'

Gently grunted. 'That proves nothing.'

'Oh, proof's another matter,' Reymerston smiled. 'You had plenty of proof against the Major, but it didn't seem to make you so very happy.'

Gently swallowed a slow draught. 'Then what are you saying?'

'I suppose it amounts to this. Once you believed me, against all the proof, when I told you what happened to the Selly woman. There was nothing against me at all, I was outside the scope of your investigation. I couldn't even produce a worthwhile motive, because in fact I didn't have one. But you believed me: without proof. You knew I wasn't telling you a lie.'

'Because you knew how she died.'

'It won't wash, old lad. I could have had that from the Major.'

Gently sieved beer through his mouth. The doubt had occurred to him, but he'd dismissed it.

'I didn't,' Reymerston said. 'The truth was I scarcely knew the man. But the possibility must have struck you. And yet you still accepted what I said.'

'So?'

Reymerston looked at him steadily. 'Now listen to me again. I didn't do for Quennell, and I don't know a damned thing about it. Neither does Ruth, as far as I know, and I'm certain she would have told me if she did.'

Gently stared at emptiness. 'And I'm supposed to accept that?'

'Oh, you'll have to go through the motions,' Reymerston said. 'Old Hawkeye out there in the car will stick to your elbow, making sure you do. But just between us, I'm trying to plant the truth, to make sure you keep your eye lifting. Perhaps professionally you daren't accept it, but at least you'll know it's on the table.'

He took a long pull, still watching Gently, whose eyes were directed towards the window. Down below, gulls were whooping behind a longshore boat that was motoring up the river. And they could just see Eyke, sulking in the car, face turned resolutely ahead. Then he vanished temporarily as he stretched over to wind down the opposite window.

'Don't forget the letter.'

'The letter's a fake.'

'At least the daughter was convinced by the handwriting.'

'Oh dear!' Reymerston said. 'What you don't know is that Ruth would never have risked a letter. I couldn't write to her and she would never write to me. We arranged at one meeting for the next. A couple of times, when something came up, she rang me. But even then it was from a box.'

'She went in so much fear of her husband?'

'Quennell was a brute, but it wasn't only that. You spoke of the daughter, and if you've met her you'll know she's a very disturbed kid. And not just over this business. A year ago she had nervous trouble of some sort. Ruth feels deeply responsible for her and she wouldn't risk an upset in the home.' He waved his glass. 'Besides, it's ridiculous! Ruth described the letter to me. No doubt there are women who write such twaddle, but you couldn't imagine it of Ruth.'

'People sometimes suit their style to the recipient.'

Reymerston stared before replying. 'If you sat where I'm sitting you'd know how stupid that idea is.'

'She must have other acquaintances.'

'Not boy friends.'

'If you, why not others?'

'Simply because.' Reymerston smiled suddenly. 'All right – it was worth an airing!' He drank. 'In point of fact, I know a woman who might write such letters. But not in Ruth Quennell's handwriting. It simply has to be a fake.'

'A woman living here …?'

Reymerston was thoughtful for a moment. Then he shrugged.

'So,' Gently said. 'If not you, if not another boy friend, who am I looking for?'

Reymerston stared over his glass. 'Don't think I haven't been giving it some thought. Unlike you, I know the field, and unlike you, I know I'm innocent. And unlike you I'm a suspect – which really gets the grey matter weaving. All the same, one doesn't rush to point a finger at other people.'

'But you can point one.'

'Maybe. In a very wavering fashion.'

'Then you'd better point it.'

Reymerston hesitated, toying with the glass.

'Well ... it's this way. I mentioned Quennell in connection with Joe Rayner. He was the same sort of hard, ambitious, opportunist sort of character. And during the last year there's been a bit of a shake-up at Tallis Press. And the long and short of it is that Quennell finished up as managing director.'

Gently sat blank-faced. 'What was he before?'

'General manager,' Reymerston said.

'Who was jumped over?'

Reymerston twiddled the glass. 'It isn't quite so simple as you're thinking. When Arthur Tallis died, last year, his brother Raymond took over the helm, then he stepped down and Quennell stepped up, with his son as assistant. Before that, in Arthur Tallis's time, Quennell wasn't even a director.'

'So you're pointing at Raymond Tallis.'

'Yes, but there's rather more to it. I tell you what – let's call in Hawkeye. He can give you the official version.'

Reymerston finished his beer, got up and went out to summon Eyke.

Gently rose too: the beer, the warmth were making his head begin to swim. Pipe in mouth he strolled to the big window with its ranging view. Could he believe Reymerston? He wanted to! And just that very thing warned him to be cautious. With puckered face he stared at the canvas, a swirling, chromatic composition. As always, Reymerston stayed an enigma, a man you had to guard yourself from liking ... perhaps, after seeing the Quennell woman, he would know better what to think.

Eyke came in sweating from his frowst in the car. He avoided Gently's eye, refused a beer and took a seat in a corner.

What he was thinking was plain enough: once more this fellow had put it over on Gently! He sat defensively, eyeing the floor, obviously waiting to hear the worst.

'Well?' Gently growled.

'Just ask the Inspector about the tragedy that happened here a year ago.'

'A year ago ...?' Eyke stared at Reymerston. 'Would that be when Arthur Tallis was lost off his yacht?'

'That's it.'

Eyke glanced at Gently: now his suspicions were fully roused! Not only had Reymerston talked himself off the hook, but he had dragged in a red herring as well ...

'That has no connection with this job, sir.'

'All the same, let's have it!' Gently snapped.

'There was nothing comic. I was at the inquest.'

'So now you can tell me what happened.'

Eyke looked as though he might have been regretting the beer.

'Well, sir, that's about what did happen. Arthur Tallis was lost off his yacht at sea. The Tallises have always been sailing people – his brother keeps a boat down at the club.'

'So give it me in detail.'

Eyke was clearly unhappy; he ran a finger under his collar. And Reymerston wasn't helping matters by sitting quizzing him with a half-smile ...

'It was September of last year, sir. They were going on a trip down to Harwich. Arthur Tallis had a thirty-six-footer, a Bermudan yawl called *Spindrift*.'

'Who went with him?'

'His brother and Quennell, Sir.' Eyke brought it out with a touch of defiance. 'They're both experienced yachtsmen who'd often sailed with Tallis before. His brother gave evidence of trips to Holland and the Baltic, let alone a jill down the coast to Harwich.'

'So.'

'They set out in the morning with a light offshore breeze. The weather was open when they sailed but then it turned to steady rain. They were sailing quietly on a close haul with the wind taking off in the rain, so the brother and Quennell went below and left Tallis doing his trick at the helm. Half an hour later they heard a sail flap and felt the boat come into the wind, and when they went out Tallis was missing and they could see no sign of him in the sea. They threw a lifebuoy over as a marker and retraced their course, then Quennell got on the radio and fetched out Shinglebourne lifeboat. The yacht and the lifeboat searched till dark but never found a trace of Tallis.'

'Wouldn't he be wearing a life-jacket?'

'Apparently not, sir. He just had on a waterproof suit. But a life-jacket did come into it, because the lifeboat picked one up in the area. It came off a yacht that had gone missing a week earlier and had the name of the yacht stencilled on it. At the inquest the lifeboat coxswain put forward the theory that Tallis may have tried to recover this life-jacket, and somehow slipped in. He'd have known about the yacht, because it had been in the news all the week.'

'He slipped overboard and simply sank?'

'Well, it's not unusual, sir,' Eyke said hotly. 'It's what you hear in half these drowning cases, even when strong swimmers are involved. The shock seems to paralyse them.'

'All the same, you would have expected him to shout.'

'I don't agree, sir. The usual pattern is just what came out at the inquest.'

And so it was, as Gently knew from an experience quite as long as Eyke's. So often with drowning cases there was this mystery about how they could happen so obscurely.

'A straightforward case.'

'But leading to a shake-up at Tallis Press.'

'Well ... yes, sir!'

Tired of his collar, Eyke had flipped it undone and loosened the tie.

'Arthur Tallis was head of the firm, and when he went it fell on the brother. But Raymond Tallis wasn't up to the job so he appointed Quennell to run it. And I can't see anything unusual in that, sir, because Raymond Tallis was never a big man in the business.'

'Would you know who the majority shareholder is?'

'I reckon Raymond Tallis is, now.'

'Now ...?'

Eyke hauled on his tie. 'Raymond Tallis married his brother's widow.'

'He did, did he?'

And suddenly one could feel a change in the atmosphere of that room, an odd tenseness. Eyke was staring with a savage expression at his feet. Reymerston was sitting very still, the half-smile lingering on his face, looking neither at Eyke nor Gently. There was a silence that seemed to be holding its breath.

'Sir, this is all codswallop!' Eyke burst out at last. 'No one's going to tell me there's a connection.'

'When did he marry her?'

'Early this year –'

'Would that be about when Quennell took over the business?'

'So if it was, sir?'

Gently shrugged. Perhaps there was nothing too special about that! Raymond Tallis might well have wanted to get rid of his business cares before he got married. To the wife of his brother.

'Where was Raymond Tallis living?'

'He was a widower, sir.' Eyke threw a malignant look at Reymerston. 'After his wife died he was living at Ferry Cottage. That's in the grounds of his brother's house.'

'Sort of en famille.'

'If you say so, sir. But I've never heard of any scandal. And she was a widow and he was a widower, so why shouldn't they hitch up?'

'Especially with such good business reasons.'

'Yes, sir, especially, I would say! So then they had most of the shares, between them, and Quennell to run the firm.'

'A tidy arrangement.'

'Well, why not, sir?'

Gently shrugged again and looked at Reymerston. As sure as he sat there, he was convinced that the painter had another card up his sleeve.

'Is this the whole story?'

'Perhaps ... not quite.'

Reymerston leaned back, his eyes amused. No doubt it had tickled him to watch Eyke on the wrong end of an interrogation ...

'Just a small point about the tragedy that wasn't brought out at the inquest – probably of no significance, but we may as well add it to the pile.'

'I was at the inquest!' Eyke growled.

'I had this from Ruth Quennell,' Reymerston smiled. 'Quennell let it out after the inquest. I doubt whether it would have affected the verdict.'

He paused, and Gently could see Eyke's knuckles paling as he clenched his fists.

'According to Quennell, when the alarm occurred he was shut

up in the toilet. That was in the fore-cabin, and of course he couldn't see what was going on. He shouted to Raymond Tallis that they had lost way, and presumably Raymond Tallis went on deck, but Quennell didn't see it. Quennell wasn't on deck till some time afterwards. In fact, Raymond Tallis could have been on deck at any time after Quennell went into the toilet.'

Eyke jumped to his feet. 'It wasn't mentioned at the inquest.'

'Obviously not,' Reymerston smiled. 'And perhaps you can't blame Quennell for wanting to keep the story simple.'

'Sir, this is a fit-up!' Eyke exploded. 'Him and Mrs Quennell have worked it up between them. It's only his word and hers – and that's just what you would expect.'

'Hold it,' Gently grunted.

'But it's a fit-up from start to finish!'

To Reymerston, Gently said: 'Did anyone else hear about this from Quennell?'

Reymerston hunched. 'I had it from Ruth, I can't tell you any more than that. It may be something, may be nothing, but in my position one can't be choosy. You asked me for an alternative, and I'm marking your card with Raymond Tallis.'

Yet ... wasn't there still something left unsaid? Gently stared into the slightly mocking eyes. Reymerston was so relaxed, his touch so light; it was impossible to get from him more than he gave. And you wanted to believe him ...

'Have you any more to tell me?'

Slowly Reymerston shook his head. 'I've done my best. Now it's up to you to dig around, old lad.'

'Don't worry, I shall do that.'

'One thing, though.' His eyes became serious. 'Go easy on Ruth. Pretend that she's innocent, then you won't be sorry later on. Ruth has been through it these last two days ... and I love her. Don't treat her rough.'

Gently only nodded; he rose. Reymerston came with them to the door. Eyke was still fuming as they walked to the car, but catching sight of Gently's expression, stayed silent.

3

And in silence they drove along Hare Lane to its junction with the sloping green, and so back to the village street and parking at The Gull, already well filled. Then Gently said:

'I take it that we know Raymond Tallis's movements for that afternoon?'

Eyke flushed and stared fiercely at a family party just decanting from an Allegro: the man, colourfully dressed in beach gear, caught the look, winced and stared back indignantly. Eyke waited for him to lock up and shepherd his brood into The Gull. Not looking at Gently, he replied:

'As a matter of fact, sir, we do.'

'Well?'

Eyke turned goadedly. 'Look, sir! I don't know what Reymerston said to you in private, but my bet is it was a lot of flannel that he knew I wouldn't buy. Raymond Tallis has never come into it. There isn't a blind reason to sus him. His wife took the Quennell girl shopping, that's all the connection with it *he's* got. I haven't talked to him, because there was no reason to, and nothing I've heard since alters that.'

'But you do know his movements.'

'All right, sir, I do. But that was something by the way. I rang the yacht club secretary about Quennell and he happened to mention Tallis too. Tallis was due for line duty but excused himself at the last moment – a bit of property he'd had the chance to look over. That meant that Quennell should have taken over the duty.'

'Another last-minute cancellation.'

'I don't see you can make a lot of that, sir.'

'Where was the property?'

'At Welbourne, six miles off.'

'Which means that he too must have passed by where it happened.'

'But so must everybody else, sir. There's only the one road in and out.'

'The list so far reads Tallis, Mrs Tallis and Quennell's daughter, and Frank Quennell, with Reymerston chalked in.'

Eyke glowered at a fresh set of lunchers, who this time luckily failed to notice. The Gull was filling up. At the other end of the parking, drinkers clustered at outside tables beneath gay sunshades. A double-gabled, white-plastered building, the hotel had a huge corroded anchor set in flowers beneath its sign.

'Listen, sir. We're getting off the track. All this is just Reymerston flying his kite. He wants to con us into forgetting that he hasn't a leg to stand on.'

Gently gestured. 'Neither have we.'

'You can't get over that letter, sir.'

Reluctantly Gently nodded. 'But that's the queerest thing in the whole business.'

'I don't see that, sir,' Eyke said positively. 'That's the bit they can't argue away. And the more they try the plainer it gets that she wrote it and palmed it off on Quennell. Who else *could* have done that? Or would have? It comes back to her every time. And I reckon she's the one to put the pressure on. Reymerston's a clever boy, but his girl friend'll crack.'

'Once,' Gently shrugged, 'we had the Major cracking.'

'And perhaps we should have finished him, sir.'

'You still think that?'

Eyke said nothing but sat gazing at the flaking anchor.

Could you believe Reymerston? For a moment there he had a whole new plausible angle going ... you accepted his innocence, accepted his ideas and felt the case was opening out. But then, when you sat back and looked at it ... how else would a clever, guilty man respond?

In sudden repulsion from the present business he found his mind flashing back to the empty flat, a grey image out of time that wafted its smell in his nostrils. Nothing to go back to ...! He grunted:

'Well, at least let's have some lunch.'

While in Rouen, perhaps talking about him, Gabrielle and Andrée would be lunching too.

Quennell's house, The Uplands, stood in a private road that

opened off the street almost opposite Hare Lane. It was one of several pleasant houses standing well back among their trees and shrubs.

You turned through an open wrought-iron gate into a drive of granite chippings and made a sweep through rhododendrons to come out before the attractive red-brick house. Probably built in the last century, it was roofed with blue pantile, and had a row of dormer windows and a sundial over its porch. Before it ranged a lawn and flowerbeds bright with dahlias and Michaelmas daisies, about which were fluttering Peacock and Red Admiral butterflies; then behind the house, past a large brick garage, you could see kitchen gardens; while overhead spread the crown of a big copper beech.

'A few bobs'-worth here, sir ...' Eyke murmured.

Gazing, Gently felt a pang of resentment. Others could live in such homes as this while he, he was stuck with his flat and his villa at Finchley! He could imagine Gabrielle coming out of that porch, or loitering with the flowers on the perfect lawn ... but it had to stay a commuter's dream. He knew it, and the pang went deep. He growled:

'Whose is the Mini?'

One was standing on the chippings by the porch. Quennell's Rolls, no doubt, was safely cocooned behind the doors of the garage.

'That's Mrs Quennell's car, sir. The son has a TR7.'

'And the daughter just has a bike.'

'Well ... yes, sir.' Eyke sounded uneasy.

Gently parked and they got out. Doors were open right through the house; from the porch one looked down a parquet-floored hall to a bright patch of colour, a lawn at the back. There a woman was seated on a bench and beside her, on the grass, Fiona Quennell. Fiona Quennell was sitting stiffly, gazing straight ahead, but at that distance her face was a blur. Gently rang, and chimes pealed in the house; in a moment Fiona Quennell had sprung to her feet. For an instant she stood poised, gazing towards them, then she took to her heels down the lawn. The woman, who had also risen, was calling:

'Fiona, come back ... there's nothing to be afraid of!'

But Fiona didn't come back, and finally the woman made a helpless gesture. She turned towards the house, where a second woman had already appeared from a doorway.

'All right, Maudie. I'll get it.'

She came on steadily up the hall.

'That tricky bitch!' Eyke was muttering. 'We've lost her again ... at the back, there's a rear access.'

'Andrew rang telling me to expect you, but I had hoped that my son would be here.'

What one noticed first about Ruth Quennell was a timidity in her manner. Her eyes, grey-blue, met yours but then flickered away evasively: she spoke looking past you, as though catching sight of something distant.

'If you would prefer to have someone present ...'

They were entering a spacious lounge, a room panelled unexpectedly in limed oak, giving it a suave, soothing appearance. It was daintily furnished; a suite of a settee and six chairs covered in flowered cretonne; in the hearth stood a bowl of flowers, and above the hearth hung a framed photograph of a Dragon yacht.

'No, thank you. There's only Maudie, and she'll be wanting to get away.'

What you noticed next was the likeness to her daughter in the wide cheekbones, straight nose and shapely jaw. A woman in her mid-forties and not pretending to anything else; her soft hair was streaked with grey and she wore no hint of make-up. Yet she was attractive; it was difficult to place. A simple blouse and skirt merely suggested a good figure.

'All this must be very upsetting for you.'

'Please – I've done my share of crying! Now I just want to get it over. For Fiona's sake more than my own.'

'Your daughter is still disturbed.'

'Very disturbed.' Ruth Quennell's mouth quivered. 'This isn't the first time she's been upset. We've had trouble with her before.'

She seated herself at one end of the settee and, after a pause, Gently took the other. The room was fragrant: it was partly the flowers, partly a sweetness from the oak panelling. Sun entered it through tall sash windows hung with curtains in a beige velour.

'You realise how important it is to establish your movements on Saturday afternoon.'

'Yes, I realise.'

'Also your husband's movements and those of the rest of your household.'

She nodded nervously. 'I've been through it in my mind a hundred times at least. But I can think of nothing. On Saturday, everything went on as normal.'

'May I mention the letter?'

At once she was agitated, her hands creeping together on her lap. But she answered calmly:

'I can only repeat that I have never written any such letter.'

'Yet the handwriting was yours?'

'It was mine. But all the same I didn't write it.'

'Do you know anyone who can imitate your hand?'

She shook her head, her hands working.

'Andrew will have told you we never wrote letters. And never would I have written such a letter as that.'

'Would you have an example of your daughter's handwriting?'

Her eyes jumped wide in sudden dread.

'You can't be suggesting ...?'

'If I may, I would like a sight of her hand.'

Ruth Quennell was trembling; but after a moment she rose and went to a bureau. There she shuffled through loose papers to return with some sheets of foolscap. In silence she handed them to him. They were sheets of an essay, probably homework. The style of the writing was vague, incoherent; quite unlike the firm hand of the letter.

'Fiona would never do such a wicked thing.'

'But your daughter would know of your acquaintance with Mr Reymerston.'

Ruth Quennell's face was hot. 'She may have known of it, but she would never have dreamed of giving me away. You don't understand.'

'She was on your side.'

'Yes, I suppose you could put it like that!'

'But towards her father ...'

'Don't misunderstand me. Simply, there wasn't any sympathy between them.'

'She would know, of course, that you and he were estranged.'

Ruth Quennell's hands were twisting continually. 'Most of her life she's known about that, which is probably the reason she is how she is. It's never been a secret. Since Fiona was born my husband had been unfaithful to me, first with one woman, then another, at last with that woman in his employ. It got to be the usual state of affairs. In a sort of way, it was a settled household.'

'Yet your husband remained jealous.'

'Because he treated me as property.'

'Who he wouldn't let go to another man.'

'Oh ... please!'

She was trembling pitiably, the last words coming as half a sob.

'I'm sorry, Mrs Quennell ...'

'I know you have to ask me these things. But it's not what you think. I couldn't have left Fiona, and Andrew understood that.'

'Divorce was out.'

'Yes. Oh yes.'

Across on a hard-bottomed chair, Eyke stirred.

'Describe to me, if you will, the events that took place on Saturday.'

He was feeling an urgent desire to smoke, and in fact had noticed evidence of a pipe-smoker's having inhabited the room. On a stool by one of the chairs stood a large glass ashtray, while on the bars of the fire-grate nearest the chair, where you'd knock out a pipe, were a few black flakes. Quennell's chair ...? Looking around, he spotted a pot-bellied jar standing on a shelf.

'As I told you, everything was normal.'

'For example, how did your husband spend the morning?'

'Oh ... Frederick. For a time, after breakfast, he was in the study writing letters. After that he went down the garden – to pick apples, I believe. Then, just before lunch, he came in to wash and change his gear.'

'At lunch he seemed quite as usual?'

'I'm used to him being silent at table. We had little to say to each other, and I don't remember any special remark.'

'His attitude was normal.'

'Yes ... I think so.' She coloured as she added: 'To be truthful I was thinking of other matters, and wanting lunch over as quickly as possible.'

'Your son I believe was absent.'

'Frank left after breakfast.'

'What was your daughter's attitude at lunch?'

'Fiona was always nervous in her father's presence and Saturday was no exception.'

'Did they speak to each other?'

'I don't think so. Fiona was only toying with her food. Then she excused herself because she had to get ready to go out with Julie Tallis.'

Gently hesitated. 'She is friendly with Mrs Tallis?'

'Naturally.' Ruth Quennell sounded mildly surprised. 'Fiona especially. We used to live next door to them before Freddy bought The Uplands. I think perhaps Arthur Tallis was more like a father to her than Freddy was. It was when poor Arthur died that we had trouble with her before. Then there's Paul, the son. Fiona and he grew up together. He's a very nice boy, just starting his second year at UEA.'

'Your families see a great deal of each other.'

'Of course. We've always been close.'

'There would be a common bond in sailing.'

'Ray and Freddy often crewed for each other. Paul has crewed for Freddy too ... though not so often, lately. I've never taken to it, nor has Frank. And Fiona will never go near a yacht.'

'Arthur Tallis's death didn't put them off?'

'That was an accident in a thousand.'

Clearly Reymerston hadn't broached his ideas to her; her posture now was more relaxed. To her, the Tallises were an innocent subject, a relief from the trend of Gently's questions. Yet, if there were anything in it, must she not have had at least a glancing suspicion?

'Raymond Tallis appreciated your husband's business ability.'

She nodded indifferently. 'The firm was Freddy's life. Perhaps that's what led to us drifting apart. Freddy didn't really have time for a wife.'

'So Raymond Tallis stepped down.'

'Oh, Ray! Ray needed someone to replace his brother. Ray had always played second fiddle, and being leader of the band didn't suit him at all.'

'It was a natural adjustment?'

'Really, Freddy took over from the time poor Arthur went.'

Either she was a consummate actress or Reymerston's red herring was exactly that.

'Coming back to the Saturday morning. Did your husband have any visitors?'

At once she tensed again, the greyish eyes slipping past him.

'Not visitors. There was Jackson, the gardener, who was here until twelve. And Maudie comes in Saturday mornings, but Freddy didn't speak to her.'

Gently glanced at Eyke: Eyke shrugged.

'We had a word with Jackson, sir. Says Mr Quennell was with him down the garden till he left. That was after twelve, sir. Mr Quennell kept him late, making a clamp.'

'Who else visited the house that morning?'

'Just the tradesmen,' Ruth Quennell said. 'I paid the milkman and the butcher myself. The postman came before we were up.'

'Your husband had mail?'

'Two bills.'

'Would you have known if he had a visitor?'

Her hands were working. 'I was helping Maudie, first in the bedrooms, then in the kitchen. I think I would have known.'

'Where was your daughter?'

'Fiona was in her bedroom doing school-work. Then she came down here, I think ... now I remember! She was talking to Paul.'

'Paul Tallis?'

'Yes, Paul. He was going to the football at Ipswich. He invited Fiona to go with him, but she was already fixed up with Julie.'

'Paul Tallis was here?'

'Yes, I'm sorry. I tend to look on him as one of the family. He was here for about half an hour. But that was when Freddy was in the garden.'

'Just talking to your daughter.'

Ruth Quennell nodded. 'They are more like brother and sister, you know.'

Gently stared at Quennell's chair. Just the faintest strand of a connection? Or – was it? But for Reymerston he would have dismissed it out of hand ...

'So that was the morning up to lunch. Your daughter has left the table. Was the domestic present?'

'No.'

'Then we'll take it from there. And I would like times.'

Her mouth was quivering again and she was keeping her eyes on the carpet. Guilty or innocent, it must be an ordeal to have to live through those moments again. Gently had deliberately indicated the scene when, for the last time, she'd been alone with her husband: hated perhaps, but the father of her children, the companion of years, and once a lover. Across the table with the empty dishes all that had ended ... how?

'We had lunch earlier on Saturdays ... because of his sailing, you know.'

'When?'

'About twenty to one. I dare say it was over by ten past.'

'Your husband was dressed for sailing?'

'Yes. He was dressed in the way he was ... found. His sailing jacket and waterproof trousers. He kept a pair of Magisters on the yacht.'

'After your daughter left, he said nothing?'

In a small voice she said: 'Nothing.'

'He gave no indication of what he was thinking?'

Hastily she shook her head.

'Who was first to leave the table?'

'He looked round for an ashtray to scrape out his pipe. There wasn't one. So he got up and went through to the kitchen, where there is a swing-bin.'

'And then?'

'I could hear him in there ... the kitchen is just across the hall. I wanted him out of the way before I began clearing the table. But for some reason, he hung around in the kitchen for several minutes.'

'Did you see him again?'

'No.' She was trying hard to keep it matter-of-fact. 'I heard him come out again and go down the hall into the study. Then I began to clear away. I heard his car leaving ten minutes later. I was in a hurry too, you understand ...' Her mouth puckered. 'I was glad when he had gone.'

'Who was in the kitchen just before lunch?'

'Me. I was carrying things through. Then Freddy washed his hands at the sink. I was the last person in there.'

'Your daughter?'

'I didn't see her. She came down from her room, I think.'

'Then your husband left when?'

'I can't be certain, but it would be somewhere about one-thirty.'

From a pocket in her skirt she tugged a handkerchief and dabbed it to her eyes. Eyke looked uncomfortable; he shifted his feet. Ruth Quennell stuffed the handkerchief away and blinked rapidly.

'I'm sorry.'

Gently shrugged. 'Take your time, Mrs Quennell.'

'Believe me, I want to help you ...'

Why did he suddenly think of the Major?

In a moment she gave a little sigh. 'I was still washing up when Julie got here. I like Julie, she's a nice person really. But the way she dresses makes me feel dowdy.'

'Julie is Mrs Tallis.'

'Yes. Julie always had a soft spot for Ray. His first wife was rather horsy, in fact she was killed in a riding accident. It surprised no one when Julie and Ray joined up. Julie's a woman who needs a man.'

'What time did she arrive?'

'It would be about a quarter to two. She was in a hurry as well. She and Fiona were going into town to buy clothes. I offered her a cup of coffee, but she said she couldn't wait, so I called Fiona from her room and they went off straight away.'

'Did she say why she was in a hurry?'

Ruth Quennell shook her head. 'She perhaps had people she was meeting in town. Julie gets about, she has lots of friends.'

'Your daughter would be excited, going to buy clothes?'

'One would have thought so, but she wasn't.' Her eyes were distant for an instant. 'My daughter is a strange girl.'

'Did she say anything to you?'

'No. She walked straight past me out to the car.'

'Perhaps she would rather have gone to the football.'

Ruth Quennell was silent. Then she shrugged feebly.

'At what time was your assignation?'

She started, then drew herself a little straighter. 'No particular time. I would simply get to the cottage as soon as I could.' Her hands were active once more. 'Sometimes I couldn't get away promptly – when Freddy had a later race. Andrew would wait until I came.'

'But on Saturday?'

'Then I was early. I got to the cottage soon after two.'

'How soon after?'

'I don't know! Andrew had only just arrived.'

'You drove straight there?'

'Yes.'

'How far?'

'It's only about two miles. At the top of the street you turn left. It couldn't have taken me more than five minutes.'

'And Mr Reymerston was waiting.'

'Yes, I said so.'

'When you arrived his car was parked and he was in the cottage?'

'He came out – he always comes out, to help me park out of sight. He was there before me, I swear it. He had opened two of the windows.'

Now she was staring at him, eyes wide: this she must make him believe, somehow! Her cheeks were burning. Even the hands had drawn apart, clenched into fists.

And it wasn't the Major he was thinking of now: it was Gabrielle who sat facing him so anguishedly.

'What was the latest time you could have got there?'

Terror flared in her eyes. And he knew what she was thinking: though she might be innocent, wasn't it possible that he ...?

'Listen! At the most I was there by ten minutes past two. I rushed everything, I was early. Usually, I'm not there till half-past.'

'You surprised him.'

'Yes – listen. Always when I get there he has a kettle boiling. The first thing we do is make a pot of tea. And the kettle was on – it was simmering.'

'Then he had been there at least since two?'

'Yes – oh yes!'

But mustn't she realise that it didn't cover him? On her own showing he'd had half an hour to deal with Quennell and set the scene at the cottage ...

'Please believe me. Everything was normal. It was just another of our meetings. Andy was normal. We made love. Do you think I would have noticed nothing?'

Perhaps it was a good point: and one she'd have gone over again and again. If Reymerston were guilty, could he really have concealed it through the searching moments of that afternoon?

And yet ... Reymerston?

'What time did you leave again?'

She gave a soft sigh and sat back. 'At half-past four. We could never have long. To me it always seems like five minutes.'

Yes ... as with Gabrielle! 'Were you first to arrive home?'

'I met Julie there, dropping off Fiona. So of course I had to make an excuse. Frank arrived back while Julie was there.'

'What time would you have expected your husband to get back?'

'It depended on the conditions. But when he wasn't back by seven, Frank gave the yacht club a ring. So then we knew he hadn't been there and hadn't gone somewhere with his ... friend. At nine, Frank rang her too. She was just as concerned as we were.'

Also Frank Quennell had rung the works, but the nightwatchman could tell him nothing. And finally the police, the call being timed at nine fifty-eight.

'During the evening, where was your daughter?'

'Fiona went up to her room.'

'Did she seem disturbed then?'

'Perhaps she was quiet.' Ruth Quennell gave her weak shrug.

'And ... since yesterday?'

Her mouth quivered afresh. 'She's the way she was before ... at first, a complete blank, not even recognising people.'

'How long did it continue then?'

'Two or three weeks. We kept her at home for a term.'

Nevertheless he would have to talk to her. Something she knew, that was evident. In that disturbed brain there lurked a hint he needed his hand on. But not now. He stared at the woman, whose eyes were hazed again with tears.

'Then that's all, Mrs Quennell.'

'You do believe me ... and Andy?'

'I would like you to make an amended statement covering the fresh points we've brought out.'

'I must go to the police station again?'

Gently shot Eyke a look.

'I'll arrange for someone to come here, ma'am,' Eyke said quickly. 'No need for you to be inconvenienced just now.'

She saw them out and stood watching from the porch as Gently turned to drive away. He could see her in his mirror, a forlorn figure, still watching as they passed out of sight. Then he had to brake sharply to avoid a coffee-coloured TR7: the TR7 braked also and its driver scrambled out.

'Look here – I thought I warned you not to come harassing mother!'

He was a heavily-built young man with fleshy features and indignant eyes; he'd come running round to Eyke's window and thumped for Eyke to wind it down.

'I won't have you coming here when she's alone – this morning I've been in touch with our lawyers! They're making an appointment and, in any case, I'm the person you should be talking to ...'

Gently said: 'Are you Frank Quennell?'

'I'm Frank Quennell – who are you?'

Gently told him. Frank Quennell stared at him challengingly, his mouth agape.

'So they've got you on it! Well, perhaps now there'll be some progress round here. And what I'm telling you straight away is to have a chat with Uncle Raymond. This morning I saw him for the first time and his behaviour to me was highly suspicious. And he's got reasons! Listen, I can tell you some funny business about a certain inquest ...'

It was the card that Reymerston hadn't played, but left Gently to discover for himself. Frank Quennell too had heard the inside story and from his father's own lips. Proof positive: but if he'd had it from Reymerston, might he not have suspected collusion?

'What precisely are you saying?'

'I'm saying that father knew too much! I mean, look what happened. Would Uncle Raymond have handed over out of goodness of heart? It was all his, and when he married Aunt Julia ... doesn't it stand out a mile? And Uncle Raymond wasn't sailing on Saturday, neither was he at the house.'

'How do you know that?'

'Because I called there. He'd asked me to pick up a set of estimates. When I called there at four the house was deserted, and just as I was leaving he drove up.'

'Didn't he say where he'd been?'

'No, he didn't, and it would have been some cock-and-bull story. And today he was going out of his way to avoid me, not even wanting to catch my eye ...'

39

Presumably Frank Quennell took after his father, since his features bore little resemblance to Ruth Quennell's; also from that direction must have come his build, his clumsy movements, perhaps his aggression. Double his age, and that would have been his father standing in the drive and laying down the law.

'I'll bear in mind what you say.'

'Yes, you'd better. And let me tell you —'

'Meanwhile, it would be better not to bother your mother with this foolishness.'

'I — what?'

He stood gaping at Gently, who let in his clutch and drove away.

4

He drove down to the green and, parking by a phone box, sat for some moments scowling at the scene. Beside him Eyke sat straight-faced and silent, but you could feel his disapproval like the touch of frost. Gently had been too soft! Instead of wading in he had used the soft pedal all the time, treating Ruth Quennell like an innocent witness: always hesitating to turn the screw. And wasn't there some truth in it? For a moment back there it had seemed to him as though he were badgering Gabrielle ... his objectivity was slipping. From now on, was that what he had to expect?

Doggedly he stuffed his pipe in his mouth and chewed at it cold. So she was innocent, was she? Then explain how Quennell got the letter without her involvement – remembering that the critical time was between when he changed his gear and when he went to the study, no doubt to phone. You could narrow it further. He had probably had lunch with no other thought than of the afternoon's sailing. Then he had been alone with her; then he'd spent longer in the kitchen than was at all necessary to scrape out a pipe ...

Almost you could see him slipping across there and feverishly ripping open the envelope, glaring at the contents, shoving them away in the big pocket of his sailing jacket. The bitch! But he'd show her. He'd hastened to the study to ring the yacht club. Then he'd jumped in his car and driven to the spot to await her arrival.

Yet ... how could she credibly have worked the trick while they were sitting together at table – making him believe that he'd found a letter which she'd supposed had been delivered? Through Fiona Quennell? By some sly manoeuvre as the latter left the room? Between the two of them the letter had been planted, because there was no other explanation: and so innocence went out of the window. However you looked at it, guilty knowledge ...

Gently frowned: he was beginning to get a headache! And

suddenly he found himself blaming Reymerston. If he were leaning over backwards for Ruth Quennell, wasn't it just because she was Reymerston's woman? It was, he knew, and the knowledge irked him. Irritably he turned on the stone-faced Eyke.

'Use that phone box. I want the address of the property Raymond Tallis went to view.'

He could see Eyke's mouth tighten. 'Are we checking on Tallis, sir?'

'Can you think of any good reason not to?'

Either Eyke couldn't or he kept it to himself.

He sat fretting in the overwarm car while Eyke applied himself to the phone box. Finally the door of the box clunked and Eyke climbed back into the car.

'It's a house called Heatherings, sir, and it belongs to a US Airforce Colonel. He's been promoted and sent back to Washington, but his wife had stayed behind to sell the property.'

Well: it made for colour. 'Can she see us?'

'Yes, sir, the agent rang her. It seems that Tallis made an appointment to view earlier, but cancelled it and had to make another. Saturday afternoon was the soonest. The lady had been away in London with her husband.'

Gently gnawed his pipe: it sounded innocent. 'He must have been keen, to give up his sailing.'

'Oh, I don't know, sir. From what I hear, line duty isn't very popular.'

Put at its meatiest, there was half a chance that Tallis had worked the appointment to give himself an alibi ... but much more likely that he'd grabbed an excuse to avoid a tiresome afternoon. Gently grunted as he fired the engine. Yes, they would check on Raymond Tallis! But because he was playing Reymerston's game was no reason why he should lose sight of Reymerston.

'First, we'll take a look at that cottage.'

'It's a turn by the church, sir.'

'As we pass by The Uplands, check your watch.'

Eyke was beginning to look almost cheerful.

Platten's Loke was a narrow road that quickly took them away from the village. It skirted a low, marshy valley lying beneath a ridge darkly crested with pines. Followed a stretch of bracken heath where foot and bridle-paths were posted; then they could see, nested in trees, a solitary, low-roofed cottage.

'That's it, sir ... Warren Lodge.'

They parked and Eyke read his watch. From the turning to The Uplands to Reymerston's love-nest the driving time was six minutes. They got out. A gap in a hedge was all that apologised for an entry; nevertheless it was wide enough for a car, and car tracks showed in the rough grass. Gently followed them round the back of the cottage. Yes: room for two cars, beside a derelict well. Impulsively he looked down the well, to see his head mirrored, as though in black enamel, at a huge depth.

'Not many mod cons.'

'None at all, sir,' Eyke said, behind him. 'An old country boy used to live here. I doubt if they've done much to it since he went.'

Yet the cottage wasn't entirely neglected. Newish curtains hung in the windows, and, peering through them, one saw tidy rooms and inexpensive modern furniture. Lamps and a stove used bottled gas, in one room was a portable shower and a chemical toilet. Outside the structure looked sound, though moss and wall-leek clung to the tiles.

And here they had come, Reymerston and she, on the weekends when the London bloke had stayed in London, when Quennell had been occupied with his yacht and his mistress, and Fiona Quennell had been ... where? A couple of snatched, hasty hours: you almost smiled at such innocence. A pair of true lovers. Reymerston and all, how could you believe they had plotted murder?

'She would have been here by ten past two.'

'That would have given him time enough,' Eyke said quickly. 'On the lady's own account Quennell left his house not later than half one. Give him quarter of an hour to get there and park his car – he could have been dead five minutes later. Then chummie had got twenty minutes to drive round here and put the kettle on.'

'It's a tight schedule.'

'But time enough, sir.'

'Killing people is hard on the nerves.'

Eyke snorted. 'I don't know about you, sir, but I don't reckon that chummie has got many nerves.'

'Yet he did neglect to search the body.'

'Well, that was our bit of luck, sir.'

'Still ... though he was provident enough to bring away the weapon, mightn't he have been in a hurry to dispose of it later?'

Eyke checked, his eyes suddenly wary. Then colour crept into his cheek.

'You mean the well, sir?'

'Has anyone been down?'

Unhappily Eyke shook his head. 'We were concentrating on the scene, sir, and Reymerston's place. I hadn't got round to a check here.'

'Better get a team out.'

'I'll do it at once, sir. If I may use your RT.'

He hurried away to the car, leaving Gently to contemplate the cottage. A little breeze was stirring the leaves overhead, leaves dark at the end of summer. A place so quiet and seeming-remote ... the only other sound was an undertone of birds. Even on Saturday, at around two there couldn't have been much chance of any eyes on the cottage ...

Eyke returned.

'They'll be out directly, sir, with a warrant for the property.'

'Give me your opinion. If Reymerston is chummie, how far do you think Mrs Quennell is involved with him?'

Eyke's eyes were cautious again. 'Well, sir, the facts are the facts. Someone had to write that letter, and someone had to plant it on Quennell.'

'You would think her capable of it.'

'I'd say so, sir.' But Eyke was beginning to frown. 'Maybe she didn't know what he had in mind, but she must have known he was up to no good.'

'And now that she does know?'

'She's standing by him, sir. In for a penny, in for a pound.'

'You'd put your money on it.'

'Well ... yes, sir. Like I say, the facts are the facts.'

A proper corrective to his vacillations! Moodily, Gently lit his pipe. If the well yielded up what they were looking for the question would be settled, and no more doubt. And yet ... He puffed edgily, feeling his head begin to throb. Confound Reymerston!

'Come on. Let's go and talk to the colonel's lady.'

The road to Welbourne passed between tall elm hedges to emerge in heathland edged with pines. For a time green gorse billowed beside them, with stonecrop yellow at its foot, while spires of weld stood tall along the verges beside spear thistle and mullein. Then they began to see heather between gaps in the gorse; at first a few lively patches, soon whole acres curded with purple.

Shimmering bluely, the heather rolled away to the sharp green reefs of the pines, trimmed here and there with the dullness of birches or a drift of fawn grass and russet bracken. At close hand it seemed to glitter in the strong, soft sun, and its perfume, warm and honey-like, penetrated even the moving car.

'You've caught it right, sir.'

Gently was conscious of Eyke's complacent glance.

'It could almost be Scotland ...'

'Suffolk, sir. And in the spring there's gorse you wouldn't believe.'

'You'll be a local man,' Gently said.

'That's right, sir. Suffolk.'

And Gently, what was he, driving by Eyke's purple acres? Not a man of anywhere: just a travelling headache, an actor in someone else's scene ...

'This is Welbourne, sir.'

They entered a village where the road drifted down by a long green. Shy, familiar, higgledy-piggledy, the sunned houses descended with it. At the bottom a pond stubbed with willows, a shop and a couple of pubs; and further over, screened by trees, the flint and brownstone of a church.

'Welbourne ...'

'Have you been here before, sir?'

Something about the place touched a chord. And two years ago he'd been out that way on a case involving a young woman and a bird-warden.

'From Ipswich to Grimchurch, would you drive through here?'

'It wouldn't be the direct route, sir.'

'But you could do?'

'Oh yes, sir.'

And that, no doubt, was the answer.

'Which way is the house?'

'Up here, sir.'

A road rose obscurely between tidy cottages, passing at once into gorsy heath with barely a car's-width between the bushes. Wasn't this familiar too? For a short distance they were still climbing; then they came to a high brick wall with a turning beside it signed: Heatherings.

'They should have a view up here, sir,' Eyke murmured.

Gently pulled into the turning. A gravel way skirted the wall for fifty yards before bringing them to open gates. And there, through the gates, stood a picture-book house, fronting the sun with a pair of Dutch gables, its casement windows latched wide and its rusty brickwork mellowly glowing. A picture-book house! Martins twittered in the eaves and the Suffolk sky burned above it. At the front, on a lawn, a woman in slacks was playing with two children, a girl and boy.

She came across.

'I'm Sarah Jonson. Are you the policemen Jellicoe rang me about?'

For the moment Gently couldn't take his eyes off the house: he felt he must devour it, brick by brick. And at once, when he climbed from the car, he was smelling the fragrance of heather again. It was coming on a faint breeze from behind a beech hedge at the foot of the garden.

'Isn't that heather over there?'

Sarah Jonson laughed surprisedly. 'Yes, it is. But I don't suppose you've come just to talk about the heather.'

She wasn't an American. A strong-featured woman of not very much over thirty, she was eyeing him with amusement, her children clinging one to each hand.

'But haven't I seen your picture somewhere?'

Gently shrugged. Not unlikely!

'Yes, now I remember. You were the policeman held hostage with the Frenchwoman, up in Scotland.' Her stare became fascinated. 'Didn't I read you had married her?'

'Mlle Orbec is now my wife.'

'Well, for gosh sakes, as Larry would say! And here you are, turning up on my doorstep.'

He found himself grinning, he couldn't help it: the encounter had been informal from the start. They might indeed have come to talk about the heather, or anything else except the deaths of printers.

'Jason, Donna, you go and play. Mummy has to talk to these gentlemen. Jason, keep on the lawn where I can see you, and Donna, you stay with Jason ...'

To Gently she said:

'I can guess what you're here about, but first let's go in and find us a drink.'

Iced lemonade was what she offered them, poured from a jug in which the sliced lemon bobbed. The lounge they had entered looked straight down the lawn to a glimpse of a panorama, beyond the beech hedge. A room of agreeable proportions, it was furnished cottage-wise with loose-cushioned oak settle and chairs; framed maps decorated the walls and there were two bookcases, both crammed. Through the open windows one still smelt the heather and heard the burbling of martins from above.

'A fine old house ...'

Sarah Jonson nodded proudly. 'Did you notice the tablet over the porch? It was built in 1707, and selling it is going to break Larry's heart.'

She had waved them to the settle and herself had taken a chair by the window. Outside the two children sat contentedly playing some game with a length of string.

'Have you lived here long?'

'For five years. Since Larry moved from Alconbury to Bentwaters. Larry's older than me, I'm his second wife, and he was planning to live here when he retired. Then this promotion came along. He had to take it, because he's being groomed for something important in the Pentagon.'

She got up to show them a photograph of a heavy-faced man with grey, wiry hair: he was taken in uniform, on the left breast of which extended five rows of ribbons.

'Larry was a flyer in Vietnam ... now he's chairborne, of course. He's been stationed over here for ten years and never wanted to go back. His ancestors came from these parts. There are Jonsons buried in Middleton churchyard. For him, this house was like a dream come true ... twice, he turned down promotion before.' She paused to sip. 'I saw him off on Friday. He had a week's leave, and we spent it at the Connaught. And that's why I couldn't show the house till Saturday.' She stared hard at Gently. 'Am I guessing right?'

It was almost a wrench to get back to business. Seated there in the calm of that sunny room, one felt a dreamy, a timeless detachment. Grudgingly he admitted:

'We check all such details.'

Sarah Jonson gave him a thoughtful look. 'When it comes to checking details, isn't it usual to employ a subordinate?' She looked away. 'This doesn't surprise me, because I have my own thoughts about a certain person. I'm local, you know, the Doctor's daughter. I get to hear all sorts of gossip.'

'This is simple routine, Mrs Jonson.'

'But you want to know if and when he was here.'

'Perhaps a little more.'

'I can tell you one thing. He was never interested in buying the house.'

She took small sips, her eyes pondering. About everything she did there was an air of decision. A doctor's daughter: and perhaps his receptionist before she became the American's bride ...

'Do you want me to repeat some gossip?'

Gently was silent. No answer to that one!

'Then it's this. Raymond Tallis was his sister-in-law's lover a long time before the brother was drowned. Do you find that interesting?'

'You tell me it is gossip.'

'Oh, but my source is unimpeachable. I had it from a third party, a patient of my father's, who had it from Julia Tallis herself. Of course Julia Tallis may have been boasting – I know her, and she's that sort of woman. But I also know Raymond Tallis, and I wouldn't put much past him. So I've been adding two and two together since I heard about Freddy Quennell. And that's why I'm not greatly surprised to have a top policeman calling on me.'

'In fact, you are suggesting ...?'

She shook her head. 'Wondering is all I'm allowed to do. But since Freddy Quennell's death, you must admit I have some reason.'

She sat quite relaxed and all the time had been using an unstressed, conversational tone. You felt she was used to the company of men and to playing her part in their discussions. Out of nowhere he suddenly found himself asking:

'Do you happen to know Andrew Reymerston?'

'Andy?' She sounded surprised. 'I know him well. In fact we own some of his pictures. Why do you ask?'

Gently didn't answer: as yet, Reymerston's name hadn't been given to the press. Sarah Jonson observed him with careful eyes.

'Oh well – you have your secrets, no doubt! But I like Andy, and I can't think he's connected with anything as sordid as this.' She paused, but Gently stayed expressionless. 'Then perhaps we'd better get on with your enquiries. Yes, Raymond Tallis did come here, and yes, I think his coming here may well have been to give himself an alibi.'

'At what time did he arrive?'

'Let me tell you first that the game began before Saturday.'

It may have been the benign influence of the house, but Gently was feeling a regrettable lack of urgency. His headache had gone; he was sipping lemonade as cold and good as he'd ever tasted. And somehow the case had taken on an academic colouring, and become something to ponder over at leisure. Or perhaps it was the tang of the heather that had this mollifying effect ...

'You mean the earlier appointment?'

'Yes. The house has been on the market eleven days. Raymond Tallis made an appointment to view for last Thursday week, the same day that Jellicoe put it on offer. But he didn't show up. We waited in for him all the afternoon. In the evening he rang ιο apologise, giving business as an excuse, and asking if he couldn't view the house on a Saturday.'

'He specifically asked for that day?'

'For a Saturday afternoon, to be precise. According to him it was the only time he could guarantee to have free. Well, the following Saturday was out because we were going to be in London, so I arranged to see him on the day I got back.'

'It was a positive engagement.'

'For two-thirty. I was due back on Saturday morning. I saw Larry off at the base on Friday and spent the night there with friends.'

A positive engagement ... yet hadn't his excuse to the yacht club been made at the last moment?

'Was he punctual?'

She shook her head. 'And I'd rushed lunch through and everything. I'd started to think he was going to play me the same trick as before.' Her eyes were suddenly probing. 'But you, you'd know the time, wouldn't you – the time that Freddy Quennell bought it! Only, of course, you aren't going to tell me.'

He had to check a smile. 'When did he arrive?'

'It had gone a quarter past three.'

'What impression did he give you?'

'Have you met Raymond Tallis? He makes even shaking hands with him seem a furtive act. I soon saw that the house didn't interest him, but I made him go over it just the same. If you like you could say he seemed absent-minded. But he was only here for half an hour.'

'Can you remember what he was wearing?'

'A fawn anorak. And no, I didn't notice any blood-stains.'

'Did he offer an excuse for being late?'

'He said he'd been asked to vet some moorings.'

'Moorings ...?'

'That would be for the yacht club. They're always short of moorings.'

Gently brooded over his glass. The times were certainly interesting, but they didn't yet know when Tallis had left his house. It could have been that he simply hadn't bothered to be punctual and had given the first excuse to come into his head. At the same time, if the house didn't interest him, why had he bothered to turn up at all ...?

He was conscious of Sarah Jonson's inquisitive eyes.

'Well – wouldn't you say he had some questions to answer?'

Now he didn't try to repress the smile. 'You must treat these enquiries as confidential.'

'Admittedly I don't like the man, and I'm not pretending I don't have bias. But I'm not alone. There are plenty of others who have wondered about his marriage with Julia. It was only six months afterwards, remember, and his brother was lost at sea in calm weather. And Freddy Quennell was the only other man aboard. At least you can't be surprised if there's gossip.'

'Still ... you will treat it as confidential.'

She pouted for a moment, then jerked her head. 'I'm a senior officer's wife you know. I listen to gossip, but I don't repeat it.' She paused, then added slyly: 'Now tell me why you asked about Andy Reymerston.'

Blank-faced, Gently replied: 'Perhaps because he might like to buy your house.'

'Andy?' Her tone was incredulous. 'Andy wouldn't want it. He's a loner.'

'That could change.'

She shook her head positively. 'Andy has been married, did you know that? But his wife died in an accident, and since then he's lived like a recluse.'

'No gossip about him.'

'He's an artist. He lives only for his painting.'

And that was probably the popular picture of Reymerston, or perhaps one he chose to foster: a man in the shadow of a past tragedy, a painter living only for his art. Gossip hadn't reached him: such care had he taken, such caution instilled in Ruth Quennell.

And in a way it was true ...

Sighing, Gently finished his lemonade and put down the glass.

'Would you like some more?'

'No. But I would like to see over your house.'

She stared with wide eyes. 'You really do surprise one!'

'I might just happen to know of a customer.'

'Oh well ... in that case.'

'How much are you asking?'

'Eighty-five thousand. To include the furniture.'

And trailing a bored Eyke after him, he got to grips with that absorbing house, with the rooms that spread out from the lofted hall and, on the first floor, from a galleried landing. An impossible dream! But he had to live it. As though here he were encountering another self, a self soothed, calmed, expanded, slowed to the peace of this many-summered home. A manner of smiling silence pervaded it, a sensation of ripened living; if there were ghosts they were glad ghosts, offering their welcome, room by room.

'Have you anyone lined up?'

'I've had enquiries, but this isn't the easiest place to sell. It's larger than most people want and too far out to attract the commuters. Actually, there's a station not far away, but it's one and a half hours into town.'

'Any early trains?'

'One that will get you to Liverpool Street by nine.'

They went outside. At the back, kitchen gardens were enclosed by the wall; at the front, beds bright with late-summer flowers bordered the ancient velvet of the lawn. Then:

'You mentioned the heather ...'

She led them to a gate in the beech hedge. Stepping outside, you entered at once into a blueness that seemed electric. Heather,

51

studded with cushions of dwarf gorse in flower, ranged in a descending blue-purple plain, fronting a vista of fields and groves, from which rose the needle spire of a church. Eastward the heather was backed by gorse and bounded by knolls of birch; and that way the colour of the sky reflected a sea only just out of sight. Shadows behind trees were heavy, blocked by the low September sun. Martins swept the heather; then there was the murmur of bees.

'Do you think your customer would be interested?'

He daren't answer that: he daren't!

'I'm sure that Larry would agree to a commission.'

'I'll let you know,' was the best he could say.

They returned to the car, and Sarah Jonson stood with her children to wave them goodbye. Eyke, who hadn't spoken a word during the visit, picked up the handset and called in. After a few words he hung up.

'They've got a man down the well now, sir.'

And the best of luck to him. 'Anything else?'

'Yes, sir. The press have been trying to contact the Quennells.'

'So leave a man there. And keep them off me.'

'We'll do our best, sir,' Eyke said. 'We're holding back the announcement that you've been called until tomorrow.' He stared ahead. 'So do we talk to Tallis, sir?'

Silently, Gently aimed the car back towards Walderness.

5

Walderness's street ended fair and square at a shingle slide into the river, where the tide was now ebbing swiftly to reveal mud shoals and rotten piles. On a corner of the salt marsh beside the river stood one or two timber dwellings, perhaps converted from fishermen's net stores, and a shed that advertised the sale of fish. Then there were the fishermen's huts and drawn-up boats along the raised bank upstream, and a spindly jetty that drooped over the mud for the use of the foot-ferry passengers. On the opposite shore these features were multiplied, and there the longshore boats were docked; while further upstream one saw boatsheds, the premises of the yacht club, a pub and the masts of yachts.

A sea picture. But the sea itself was hidden by the marram dunes. One smelt it, or heard it in the cries of gulls who, along with sandpipers, scavenged the mudflats. Distant across the river and marsh, riding above a gorsy common, stretched the compact urbation of Wolmering with its flint tower and chalked lighthouse.

'Why would a yachtsman want to shift from here?'

Gently had driven to the very end of the street. There a notice, propped against a rotting boat, informed one that the shingle was for Turning Only. In fact there was ample parking on either side of the road, formed on a stretch of firm marsh lying between river and village. The last house, a tall, white residence standing proud behind colourful gardens, fronted river, marrams and the prospect of Wolmering: and that was where Raymond Tallis lived.

Eyke said cautiously: 'It was his brother's house. He'd maybe feel he wanted a house of his own.'

'But six miles inland?'

'It's not far to drive, sir. Perhaps he thought it was worth a look.'

Perhaps. And yet, from his windows, Tallis could see the state of the tide, check the day's conditions, read off the course signalled at the yacht club. And as far as the house went, he had made himself at home there long before his brother had died ... Caxton Lodge: their grandfather had built it, leaving to stand the pleasant cottage that went with the plot.

They were waiting for Tallis; Eyke had rung the Lodge to learn that he hadn't yet returned from the works, and though an interview with Julia Tallis on her own was tempting, Gently had reluctantly decided to forgo it. Dangerous ground; because, after all, they had little to go on but a pack of gossip. It might be that a breathing-space was not inappropriate before they tangled with the property-viewing yachtsman.

'Call in again.'

Eyke obeyed, but the exchange was brief.

'They've had a second man down, sir ... the air in the well is a bit dodgy.'

'No stilettos or poniards?'

'Nothing yet, sir.'

But they should certainly have found it by now. Whatever debris had collected in the well, something thrown in on Saturday would be sitting on top of it. And, in any case ...

'What I want from the lab is a little bit of imagination! Ask them to experiment with butcher's meat – anything to get us a lead on the weapon.'

The truth was that, sitting there brooding, he was becoming more and more aware of the blind alleys in the case. The weapon was one, but whatever the direction you were brought up short in some way or another. Nothing to get one's teeth into; just a fabric of circumstance, lacking a loose end to nag away at. And the one weak strand, Fiona Quennell, beyond the reach of interrogation. What they needed was a break, a piece of solid evidence to use as a lever to set things working. But what they had was unsupported tattle, plus a suggestion from the principal suspect ...

Already it was beginning to feel like one of those cases, so apparently straightforward, that nevertheless lose momentum and finish up in the files.

'Sir.'

A plum-coloured Daimler had appeared from the direction of the village and was turning into the gravel sweep between the flowerbeds of Caxton Lodge. It stopped before a multiple garage and a thickset man got out. As he was reaching a briefcase from the car, he was joined by a woman from the house.

'She's telling him we're due to call ... she must have missed him when she rang the works.'

The man turned to stare in their direction; then he shrugged and said something to the woman. Together they went into the house, he with his hand on her waist.

'We go, sir?'

'Let him get in.'

At that instant the RT buzzed. Eyke took it, listened and hung up, his glum face even glummer.

'They've finished with the well, sir.'

'And?'

'Just some broken pots and a rusty bucket. They're still going over the cottage, but they've found nothing comic so far.'

And neither would they. With sudden conviction, Gently knew that Reymerston would leave no clue. He hadn't panicked before, and he wouldn't have done this time: the sea was his confidant when it came to evidence.

On such a tide as was now ebbing, and under Gently's own eyes, he had lost the one object that could have tied him to Vivienne.

'I was expecting your visit, Superintendent. To be frank, I'm surprised that you haven't called sooner.'

They had been shown into a drawing-room furnished neo-Victorian, with overstuffed, deep-buttoned settee and chairs. A vast Turkey carpet covered the floor and on the walls hung gloomy paintings in fresh-gilded frames; a bureau-bookcase contained books on collecting, and china trinkets stood about on small tables and whatnots. There was also a sofa, placed in a window: it had a scroll-carved mahogany frame.

'Naturally I am delighted that a man of your standing has taken charge. But, as the person most concerned with Frederick's affairs, I would have expected you to consult me earlier.'

Furtive was right: Raymond Tallis had eyes that watched you from between narrowed lids. A heavy, round-shouldered, short-necked man with plump, over-fed features, he had a shifty air built into him, making you resent his fruity tones. He had shaken hands with a grasp intended to be firm but giving only a damp, rubber-like impression.

In the hall, Gently had noticed a photograph of the two brothers and Quennell in yachting gear. Arthur Tallis had been taller, more ascetic; you might have thought it was Raymond Tallis and Quennell who were the brothers.

'I expect the Superintendent wanted to see the family first, dear.'

Julia Tallis had accompanied them in; she had gone across to the sofa and draped herself there decoratively.

A woman of interesting figure and wide-mouthed good looks, she spoke with a sexy, contralto voice in which there was a trace of local broadness.

'All the same, my dear, I would have thought it advisable to talk to me first.'

'Perhaps he didn't want to bother you at the business.'

Raymond Tallis hoisted his round shoulders.

'Please sit down.'

He himself remained standing in front of the big marble mantelpiece. He glanced towards a drinks cabinet, then felt in his pocket for a cigar-case.

'Smoke?'

Gently shook his head.

'So where would you like me to begin? I knew Frederick all his life – went to school with him, if it comes to that. A brilliant man, and tough. That's why we put him in charge at the Press. The industry is going through a revolution and you need a ruthless touch now and then.' He lit a cigar, his eyes slitted. 'Of course, I know about Ruthy and her painter! It's the sort of thing that might have upset Frederick, though he was no plaster saint himself. And Ruthy is one of those don't-touch-me women who fall hard when they do fall. But I can't see it. If it had happened in a quarrel, now ...' He puffed firmly once or twice. 'You want to know about the business, don't you?'

Expressionlessly, Gently said: 'Whatever you can tell me.'

'Yes – well.' Tallis squinted through smoke. 'The business is the obvious place to look. Frederick made changes, promotions, may have trod on a few toes. Then we've had a fight on with the unions over the introduction of new technology – not that it's ever come to blows! But things like that you'll have to consider.'

'Quennell may have made enemies?'

'It's possible, isn't it? Printers are a rum set of people.

Craftsmen, jealous of their trade. There could be one of them round the twist. Of course, I can't mention any names – there are seven hundred employees to pick from. But there are fifty redundancies coming up, and it might be worth while to take a look at those.'

'But no names.'

'Well, there you are.' Tallis took a few more quick puffs. 'I'm doing my best to put you in the picture. What else is it you want to know?'

'About Marilyn, perhaps,' Julia Tallis suggested, with a throaty little chuckle. 'Some way-out boy friend of hers may have had a rush of blood.'

Tallis brushed it aside in smoke. 'What I want is to give you every assistance. Freddy was a friend. We'd been together through thick and thin all our lives. If I can help, just say the word. I want this business cleared up fast.'

Gently hunched, staring at Tallis. 'Perhaps one of you can help me in this way,' he said. 'What I need are witnesses who passed the gorse circle at around two p.m. on Saturday.'

'At around two p.m. ....'

The Tallises exchanged looks.

'Well – I suppose I did,' Julia Tallis said. 'I was driving into town about then, but I certainly didn't see anything suspicious.' She glanced at her husband. 'Did you, Ray?'

Raymond Tallis coughed. 'No ... I didn't! But it was later when I went by – nearer three than two, I'd say.'

'But you left before me.'

'I had business here. It was near enough three when I left the village.'

He coughed again, looked round for an ashtray and stubbed the part-smoked cigar. He couldn't help it: he had a shifty air. It came into whatever he did.

'So you passed at about three,' Gently said.

'Yes, about then,' Raymond Tallis conceded. 'I can't be exact. I'd been to look at some moorings that a man was offering to the yacht club.'

'You had an appointment with him.'

'No appointment. Royce is a farmer, he'd have been in Norwich. I went to check the banks and the depth of water. I suppose I was around there for over an hour.'

'How far from the gorse circle?'

'Oh ... a mile, maybe. Nowhere that I could see it.'

'Did you see anyone?'

'Not a soul. The moorings are upstream from the harbour.'

Did he realise he'd just blown an alibi? With Raymond Tallis it was difficult to tell. He would always squint at you with narrowed eyes, giving you the impression he was putting one over. He was wearing a dark grey business suit that looked like a sack on his heavy body; he stood feet apart, hands behind him, rocking slightly under Gently's scrutiny.

'Anyway ... I didn't see anything. Either going or coming back. That would be an hour later, give or take. I'd gone to view a house at Welbourne.'

'A house ...?'

'One that took my eye when I saw the advert in a paper. Normally I'd have been sailing on Saturday, but that was the only time the owner could see me. I did try to view it earlier, but some union trouble blew up to prevent it.'

Did he need to explain that?

'The house must have been attractive to make you consider leaving here.'

'Oh Ray was never serious,' Julia Tallis smiled. 'It's just that the Tallises came from Welbourne, and Ray always has a hankering for the place. But this house suits us too well – besides which, his grandfather built it.'

'It was here you lived with your first husband.'

'Arthur – yes.' Her smile faded. 'I suppose you've heard how I lost him. I'll never understand this obsession with sailing.'

'He was an experienced yachtsman.'

She nodded.

'Lost in calm weather, I believe?'

'That's just what puzzled everyone – ' She broke off, throwing a dismayed look at her husband.

For a moment Raymond Tallis rocked in silence, then he gave an ingratiating chuckle. 'I think it's time for a drink. I don't know about you gentlemen, but I always appreciate a drink about now ...'

Gently said nothing. Julia Tallis looked vexed.

Raymond Tallis went to get the drinks.

'I was talking to Mr Frank Quennell.'

'Ah ... him!'

Now Raymond Tallis had chosen to sit. His bulk filled one of the overstuffed chairs as though it might have been designed with him in mind.

The room had windows north and east, looking out on a scene irradiated by sun, but was itself a gloomy apartment, unhelped by a wallpaper of red flock pattern.

'Frank has got his knife into me, though I'm hanged if I know why. I was telling Julie. From the way he behaves, you'd think I was responsible for what has happened.' He took a gulp of sherry.

'What's he been saying?'

'He seemed rather a confused young man.'

'Something about me?'

Gently inclined his head. 'I don't think Frank Quennell is to be taken seriously.'

Looks passing between husband and wife! Then Tallis leaned forward in his chair.

'Listen, Superintendent. I'm a man who likes to have the cards on the table. You mentioned Arthur. I can guess the rest, just what young Quennell has been telling you. Well, there's nothing in it. It was Freddy's idea, to keep the inquest short and sweet. Julie knows. We didn't want the press making a meal of a distressing business.'

He was thrusting his glass towards Gently, his eyes this once wide open. So why couldn't you accept his proffered sincerity, feeling only that it was an act?

'It was Quennell's idea ...?'

'Exactly. I would have blurted out the whole story. I was lying on a bunk with a magazine when Freddy sang out that we were in irons. For a moment it didn't sink in, then I was out of the cabin fast. But Arthur had vanished. That's the plain truth. We were bobbing about in empty sea.'

'How long before Quennell joined you?'

'Heaven knows – I was bawling my head off. But he was out pretty soon afterwards, a minute at most, I'd say.'

'And it was Quennell's idea ...'

'I repeat, yes. When we were waiting for the lifeboat to arrive. We'd better keep our tale simple, he said, or it might be all over the Sunday papers.'

'Quennell was a man of prudence.'

'You could rely on Freddy not to lose his head.'

'Which perhaps accounted for his promotion.'

Tallis stared, his eyes gone narrow again.

Julia Tallis said: 'Freddy did it for my sake. That's all there is about that. If there had been anything fishy about it, would Freddy have let it out to young Frank?'

'It was certainly confidential information.'

'And now Frank's trying to pump it up.'

His eyes vacant, Tallis said: 'We'll have to have a word with young Frank ...'

But suddenly the atmosphere had changed in that room with its fussy furniture and knick-knacks, as though the temperature had dropped a few points, or a door had opened to admit a draught. No one was drinking. Julia Tallis sat frowning, her glass beside her. Raymond Tallis squinted on at nothing, glass disregarded in his hand. A change of temperature: and no one making an effort to disguise the fact.

Gently said: 'Something else you might help with. I need a current example of Ruth Quennell's handwriting.'

Both stared at him at once. Julia Tallis said: 'I suppose you're not suggesting ...?'

'Have you any examples?'

'What if we have?'

Raymond Tallis snapped: 'This is getting past a joke! Everybody knows about the letter and that Ruth swears she never wrote it. So what are you getting at?'

'You know about the letter?'

'Do you think we haven't been round to see her? Who else would she have to turn to in a spot of bother like this?'

'You are frequently at The Uplands.'

'Good lord, we live in and out of each other's pockets. We have done all our lives. Are you going to make something out of that?'

'If the letter was a forgery, someone planted it.'

Julia Tallis said quickly: 'Well, it wasn't me. Freddy had left by the time I got there. In fact, I saw his car going up the street.'

Gently turned to Raymond Tallis. 'But you, didn't you leave earlier?'

'What if I did? I didn't call at The Uplands – nor I didn't see Freddy, then or at any time.'

'Yet that letter was planted.'

Tallis's stare was baffled. He gazed at Gently, then at his glass.

'Oh, this is all nonsense!' Julia Tallis exclaimed angrily. 'How can you suspect us of any such thing?'

'I think I should see my lawyer,' Raymond Tallis said. 'I don't like the way this is going at all. You are making fantastic allegations – apparently only on grounds supplied by Frank Quennell.'

Shrugging, Gently said: 'Can you prove your movements – between one-thirty and three p.m. on Saturday?'

'Haven't I just told you – !'

'But can you prove them?'

Tallis tried to stare him down; he didn't succeed.

'It amounts to this,' Gently said. 'If the letter was a forgery, then it was introduced from outside. The most likely person to have done that was a person familiar with The Uplands' household. Mrs Tallis perhaps had no opportunity. You yourself may have had opportunity. But I have heard of a third member of the family who seems to have had an excellent opportunity.'

Julia Tallis's hand went to her mouth. 'Paul!'

'Look, this has gone far enough!' Raymond Tallis burst out. 'I won't have you bullying my nephew and probably putting words into his mouth.'

'Where is your son, Mrs Tallis?'

'Paul has gone back to college.'

'I shall need his address.'

She looked helplessly at Tallis, whose plump features had sagged.

'Listen ... I won't have my nephew harassed!'

'I want only a few words with him, Mr Tallis.'

'I refuse to give you his address.'

'No doubt the university administration will oblige.'

'I shall forbid them.'

Gently stared blank-faced. This was certainly getting interesting! He had thrown in Paul Tallis as a matter of routine, and the reaction was quite unexpected. Even Eyke was beginning to sit up, his wry nose scenting blood.

'I understand your son paid a visit to The Uplands at some time on Saturday morning.'

'The surprise would be if he didn't,' Julia Tallis said rapidly. 'He and Fiona have a thing together. They've been close since they were kids, they went to the same junior school. When Paul's at home, if he isn't over there, then Fiona is over here. And Paul crewed for Freddy. And he's a favourite with Ruth. So where else would you expect to find him?'

'But he was there.'

'All right, he was! But only to invite Fiona to go to the match with him. Since the Town have begun the season so well, Paul has decided he's a fan.'

'That would be mid-morning.'

'Yes, I suppose so. I don't remember what time he left. He had to drive in, then get some lunch. I expect it was around eleven.'

'As far as we know, your son was the only visitor at The Uplands before lunch on Saturday.'

'Well, I didn't give him any forged letters to deliver – and nor did Ray. You can depend on that.'

'I still need his address.'

She jerked her head away and stared out at the bright-lit scene. In her agitation the broadness in her speech had become more and more marked. A village girl who had married her boss? Her handsome features were still striking. She half-sat, half-lay on the sofa in a pose that was probably habitual.

'All right, since you'll find out anyway. He's got a flat in Bancroft Road, 25E. It's off the top of Unthank Road.'

'Is there a phone number?'

'No.'

'Oh God!' Raymond Tallis copped back his drink. All the same he was looking pale, the beard-shadow prominent on his cheeks.

'He had to have it, Ray.'

Raymond Tallis shook his head: much of the starch seemed to have gone out of him. Almost you began to feel sorry for him, so unhappy did he look.

'Listen, Superintendent ... you've got to know something.' His eyes were puckering, as though in pain. 'Paul ... he's a good lad. But somehow we don't get on together.' He writhed his shoulders. 'You must know how it is – a man of the world, with your experience. For all I know you've a son of your own, one you wouldn't like questioned about his father! And Paul ... we don't hit it off.' He writhed again. 'Because of Julie and I. He blames me, you understand? It's natural enough, when you think about it.'

'He perhaps blames you for his father's death?'

'No! Oh lord, I'm not saying that. But he could do ... It's just that from the way he behaves, you'd think he hated me.'

'Paul worshipped his father,' Julia Tallis said. 'What happened was a great shock. But I'm sure he doesn't blame Ray for that. Simply he can't accept him in Arthur's place.'

Raymond Tallis kneaded his glass. 'He won't talk to me,' he said. 'After the wedding he moved into the cottage. He doesn't want to see or know I exist. He spent more time with Freddy than me.'

'He'll get over it, Ray,' Julia Tallis said. 'He's in a foolish phase, but it'll pass. He's only nineteen. We must give him time. Perhaps we shouldn't have married until the year was out.'

'Just now Paul hates me.'

'Give him time.'

'You don't know what he'll say if he's questioned.'

'Ray, you can trust Paul.'

Raymond Tallis shook his head. 'Even before this ...' He humped his shoulders.

Then his shifty eyes met Gently's.

'You must be able to see how it is! Only give him a hint of what's expected, and as likely as not he'll play along. I'm not saying he's bad, but he's got it in for me and wouldn't mind stirring up a bit of bother. As for what goes on inside his head ...' His clutch on the glass tightened.

Was the agitation genuine? That was just the problem – one would never be certain with Raymond Tallis! Automatically you distrusted him, looking for the man behind the act. His misfortune, it might be; but nothing he did seemed completely straightforward.

'I'll remember what you tell me.'

'He could even be in league with young Quennell.'

Gently stared. 'Are they also close friends?'

'I can see them ganging up on me now ...'

'Paul isn't a particular friend of Frank's,' Julia Tallis said smoothly. 'He and Frank have different interests. Frank doesn't sail, he plays golf ...' She broke off. 'Oh, look – there's Fiona at the gate!'

She sat up straight, and waved. Gently turned sharply to look down the sweep. Fiona Quennell was standing with her bicycle, staring up at the house and the windows of the room. The same blank face and dark eyes and motionless, stock-still posture: the gaze was piercing the dullness of the windows and fixed on the people seated within.

'I'll call her in.'

Julia Tallis rose, but it was as though she had startled a nervous bird. At once Fiona Quennell jumped on the bicycle and began furiously to pedal away.

'Oh, dear … that poor girl.'

Julia Tallis stood watching her out of sight.

'I'm so sorry for her. And there's nothing one can do. Ruth is the only person she'll let near her.'

'I'm told it was seeing the letter that disturbed her.'

'Yes, the sight of her mother's handwriting.'

'Couldn't it perhaps have been the letter's contents?'

After a moment, Julia Tallis said: 'I haven't seen the letter.'

Raymond Tallis was pouring another drink. No doubt about it, his face was pale. There didn't seem very much left to say. Gently set down his glass, and they went.

6

'So what do we make of all that, sir?'

A few minutes later they were back at The Gull, where as yet the parking was empty and the outside tables deserted. The sun had lost itself behind the village, escaping only here and there between long shadows; but still it lit the marram dunes and yellowed the sea visible between them. From the green, a line of visitors' cars had departed: it was a moment when the village seemed to pause.

Gently sighed – what could one make of it? The essence of the business remained unchanged. As with Reymerston, so with Tallis: you were faced with a question of credibility. In the absence of evidence, it went without saying – a scrap relating to either could change the whole picture. But as it stood you were left conjuring with motive and opportunity, and trying to convince yourself that one or other of them ...

Mechanically he filled his pipe and puffed smoke through the open car-window. You could perhaps believe it of Tallis, if the pressure building up on him had been enough! Suppose something comic about the yachting tragedy – now, of course, beyond eliciting – and Quennell had a powerful lever to bend Tallis to his will. Managing control of the firm he'd got; a majority share-holding he might want; and what else was there? Could it have been the woman who draped herself so winningly on the sofa? He took quick puffs. No doubt about one thing: Julia Tallis had a glad eye. Though married to the boss, she'd carried on with his brother, and probably it hadn't stopped there. And Tallis, the fool, was infatuated with her, that was pretty obvious too: and if she had flashed a green light, and Quennell had responded, might that not have pushed Tallis over the edge? If, if! Yet from nowhere he was remembering a delicate hesitation of Reymerston's – he knew, he'd said, a woman who might write such letters as that found on Quennell, but had declined to go further. Julia Tallis. You couldn't have invented a style that might suit her better ...

'Sir, you nailed his alibi to the wall.'

But that was going to be the least of the problems.

'And he was properly scared when you mentioned his nephew. I reckon that youngster has got something on him.'

'About the letter?'

'What else, sir?'

Gently drew and exhaled a long blast. 'Can you see Paul Tallis willingly involved in a plot against Frederick Quennell?'

'They might have kidded him along about it, sir.'

'So why is he silent now?'

'His mother might be implicated.'

'Mrs Quennell is a suspect. At least you'd think he would drop a hint.'

'Well, I don't know, sir,' Eyke put on his stubborn look. 'Young Tallis was the only visitor that morning. It was after he was there that Quennell got the letter, and I'll swear that Miss Fiona had a hand in it.'

'She too in a plot against her father?'

'It's obvious she didn't know what was in it, sir. That's why she went off the rails later.'

'And still not a whisper from Paul Tallis.'

But the fact was that, like it or not, they couldn't tie the letter to Paul Tallis. It could well have been introduced at The Uplands at a time prior to Saturday morning. More likely it had passed directly to Fiona Quennell, if she it was who had worked the plant, in one of the visits she was quoted as making so frequently to Caxton Lodge. There was evidence of recent contact between her and Julia Tallis in the shopping trip they had arranged: what more likely occasion to prime her in some way, and provide the letter? Yet ... how was she primed? What clever lie could possibly have achieved her innocent compliance?

Whoever forged or provided the letter, you stubbed your toe against that.

Eyke, who must have been thinking along the same lines, said: 'Sir, you keep coming back to Mrs Quennell. If Miss Fiona didn't pass the letter, then my guess is she saw her mother pass it.'

Yes: but where did that lead them?

'Are you suggesting a conspiracy between Mrs Quennell and the Tallises?'

'It would have suited her book, sir. You don't fancy

Reymerston, and there's nobody else in the picture.'

Gently smoked hard – a logical angle! It took care of the difficulty about Fiona Quennell: on the one side her mother, seeking her freedom, on the other Raymond Tallis his delivery from Quennell. No doubt Ruth Quennell had guessed his predicament, while he was well aware of hers: then one day it had occurred to them that the same solution met both their problems. So they had plotted ... this? Once again, the impalpable question of credibility! Where Tallis was involved, wouldn't you rather be looking for one of those accidents at sea ...?

'This evening I'll talk to young Tallis.'

'Yes, sir. Would you like me to advise Norwich?'

Gently shook his head. 'Just a quiet talk. The less we show our hands the better.'

Eyke pondered glumly for a moment. 'What we need now is a break, sir.'

'Paul Tallis may be it,' Gently said.

From Eyke's face, you could rarely tell what he was thinking.

As 'Mr Scott' – his favourite alias – Gently had booked into The Gull at lunchtime; and now, after a wash, he ordered himself an early meal. He requested a copy of the local paper and glanced over the sports page while he ate. Then, as the dining-room began to fill up, he went out again to his car.

By now it was fully dark, though a big red moon rode on his left. To Norwich was an hour's drive through a swelling country of field and plantation. One scarcely touched on a village after passing through the narrow streets of Stansgate, and traffic was scarce, though the road was a link with the seaside town of Lothing. At last, from the brow of a rise, he could see the glittering spread of the city, and soon he was coasting down a descent into an outlying suburb village.

Norwich was familiar; by the inner link road he reached the Chapelfield and Earlham roundabouts, then, cruising along Unthank Road, found the turn-off to Bancroft Road. He drove down to it: it was a short road serving as a link to three cul-de-sac streets. Number 25 was a large detached house facing a gap where steps descended. Cars, many dilapidated, lined the pavements, and lights showed in most windows: flats and bed-sitters. At nearby Earlham lay the concrete sprawl of the University.

With some difficulty Gently found parking in the gap by the
steps, then he crossed the road to the porch and double doors of
25. He went in. Bicycles were crowded in a red-and-white tiled
hall, notices were sellotaped to doors, stairs ascended a narrow
stair-well. He climbed the stairs to a lumber-stacked landing,
found a notice pointing to more stairs; and came finally to a
narrow landing lit by a single, unshaded bulb.

'Yes – you wanted me?'

At an open door a young man had been watching him climb
the stairs. Light from the room aureoled his tousled blond hair
and silhouetted a slim but strong-boned build.

'Are you Paul Tallis?'

'That's me.'

'Your mother gave me your address.'

'My mother! Is it to do with –?'

'Let's go inside where we can talk.'

The young man fell back, and Gently ered a room cluttered
with a desk, books and hi-fi equipment; not very large, it had
slanted ceilings to a dormer with two small windows. Curtains
were undrawn. One looked out on the steps and a glimpse of
street below them, then beyond to a wide suburban panorama in
which mingled the darkness of trees.

'At least you have a view, up here ...'

'I know about that. But who are you?'

'Me? Just a copper tying up some loose ends.'

'Oh – you're a policeman.'

'Do shut the door.'

Why did he suddenly feel so complaisant, like a member of the
family come on a visit? Pure sentimentality, perhaps, the sight of
this young man's first steps in independence! The desk in the
dormer, the books, the litter, the one chair, picked up at a second-
hand dealer's ... and somewhere else, no doubt, would be an iron
bedstead, with a sleeping-bag and clothes strewn about just
anywhere ...

Taking the one chair, he couldn't help asking:

'Are you settling in all right?'

Paul Tallis was staring at him uncertainly. The hair, the blue
eyes obviously came from his mother, and from his father the
smallish, high-cheekboned features.

'Look – has anything happened? I mean, if mother sent you –'

'She merely gave me your address.'

'Then ... is it Fiona?'

Gently shook his head. 'Find somewhere to sit. I just want to talk.'

'But what's it about!'

'Nothing to get alarmed over. There's always routine to clear up in matters like this.'

Paul Tallis stood staring for another moment, then cleared a corner of the desk and sat. He was dressed in a denim jacket and slacks and a shirt wide open at the neck. About him there was a healthy, fresh-air appearance; he moved with a coltish sort of grace. Now, sitting aslant on a corner of the desk, he produced a shy smile.

'All right, then! But who are you?'

Gently told him who he was.

'My goodness. When you're an important man, they pull out the stops, don't they?'

Gently grinned. 'You liked Mr Quennell?'

'Yes, I think you can say that. He was Uncle Fred, you know. There's no relationship, but we've always carried on as though there were. It was a bit difficult.' He glanced timidly at Gently. 'But I expect you know the ins and outs! I had to try to play the friendly neutral, because I've always been fond of Auntie Ruth too.'

'It couldn't always have been easy.'

'No, it wasn't. I suppose it seemed natural to a man like him, and in a way you could sympathise with him. He was a boss-man, a real tycoon. Perhaps Auntie didn't go in for enough charisma.'

'His daughter couldn't have approved much, either.'

'Fiona. No.' Paul Tallis dropped his eyes. Then they jumped back quickly to Gently's. 'Fiona is all right, is she?'

'She is still disturbed.'

His eyes were intense. 'She wouldn't let me near her, yesterday.'

'Did you try to talk to her?'

'Yes, of course. But she simply ran out of the room.' His eyes were penetrating. 'She'll be all right, will she?'

'I'm no expert,' Gently shrugged.

Paul Tallis hung his head. 'I expect they'll have told you about us.'

'I'm told you grew up together.'

'It's more than that,' Paul Tallis said bitterly. 'She's like the sister I didn't have – you knew mother had a daughter too, did you? She would have been the same age as Fiona. Fiona's more my sister than she's ever been Frank's. I shall marry her, of course. There's no one else. But now this frightful thing has happened.' He jerked up suddenly. 'Have you talked to her?'

'To her mother and brother,' Gently said.

'But not to her?'

'Not yet to her.'

His head sank again. 'Perhaps she'll never get over it.'

Below a car passed, and there was sound of more distant traffic; yet the room had an odd silence, tucked up in the roof of that Victorian house. A high room in a high house, it gave a feeling of being suspended in the night.

'I believe she has had nervous trouble before.'

'Yes. At the time when my father was drowned.'

He said it in a flat voice, his eyes on the naked boards of the floor.

'She was fond of your father.'

'Yes. Father treated her like a daughter too. She belonged to us. But that time she wasn't as bad as she is now.'

'His death was a shock.'

'She's never quite got over it.'

'To you too.'

Paul Tallis said nothing.

'And of course your mother.'

After a moment, he gave a deep sigh. 'You've spoken to her, you say. That means you know all the background! Well, don't think I blame her for a moment. I'm very fond of my mother. She was upset, yes, but perhaps what she did was the best thing for her. She needed someone, and she's got someone. And that's all there is to it, for me.'

'You feel no resentment.'

He shook his head.

'Yet I'm told that, after the wedding, you moved into the cottage.'

'Oh, that.' He kept gazing at the floor. 'It seemed a good thing to do at the time. They'd like to have the house on their own, wouldn't they, and perhaps I felt I'd like to be alone too. Anyway, the cottage is mine – or will be when I'm twenty-one.'

'Were you at the wedding?'

His shoulder twitched. 'In a way, you could say I wasn't invited. It happened on a weekday during term, when I was stuck with an exam. But it was just a registry-office affair. Only Uncle Fred was present. Then they spent a week in Torquay.' His mouth twisted. 'Really, it didn't change anything very much.'

'Not your attitude towards your Uncle Raymond?'

He looked up. 'What's he been saying?'

Gently didn't answer. Paul Tallis stared at him, blue eyes suddenly intent again.

'If you ask me, it's the other way about! Uncle Ray feels guilty and resents me.'

'Guilty of what.'

'Well – everything. Of stepping into father's shoes. Six months after father was drowned Uncle Ray had taken over the lot.'

'And that didn't bother you?'

He jerked his head. 'I'm not pretending I didn't feel it.' He glanced at a framed photograph of Arthur Tallis, the single picture that hung in the room. 'Father was a special person. Nobody could replace him. But he was gone. Mother needed some support, and I suppose father's brother was the next best thing. Well, Uncle Ray is no favourite of mine, but he was mother's choice, and I was ready to accept him. So I don't know what he's been saying, but the hostility isn't on my side.'

'For example, Miss Quennell had no wild ideas?'

Paul Tallis was silent for several moments. He'd averted his face from Gently, but the tight drag of his mouth was visible.

'Is this about the inquest?'

Gently said nothing.

'All right, then! Fiona did hear something odd about that.' He jammed his hands into the pockets of the denim jacket. 'And she does have queer ideas.'

'About your uncle?'

'It was nonsense, of course ... she was terribly upset just then. She thought that Uncle Ray was somehow to blame. But you can't take her ideas seriously.'

'How to blame?'

'I don't know! That he deliberately got rid of father.'

'Because of something she'd heard from Mr Quennell?'

'Yes, I suppose so. It had to be that.' He got up suddenly,

tormentedly. 'Look, all this is utter rot! I know Fiona, she's always romancing – and when she's upset there are no bounds to it. You can't take her seriously. I never did. I'm sure Uncle Ray did his best to save father. And Uncle Fred knew it. He was on the spot. I don't blame Uncle Ray for a thing.'

'The tragedy made no difference to their relations?'

He hesitated. 'If anything it brought them closer. Uncle Ray made Uncle Fred boss at the Press, and Uncle Fred was the only witness at the wedding.'

'Just so,' Gently said.

Paul Tallis stared at him. 'Are these the loose ends you're trying to tie up?'

Gently made a humoursome face. 'Not entirely! But it's always as well to have the whole picture.' He brought out his pipe. 'Do you mind if I smoke?'

Paul Tallis gazed at him a little longer. Then he relaxed his tense pose and dropped down again on the corner of the desk.

'All this is new to me – being put through it by a top policeman! I tell you what, I was going to make some coffee. Would you like some too?'

'Why not?' Gently said.

A door opened into a kitchenette-shower-room, in the slanted ceiling of which yawned an uncurtained skylight. Beside a bald sink stood a miniature cooker and on some shelves a minimum of crockery. Paul Tallis plugged in an electric kettle and stood two beakers on the draining-board. From a carton, one of several, he took a jar of instant coffee and measured spoonfuls into the beakers. From the doorway, Gently watched.

'How long have you been here?'

'Only since yesterday. Actually, you're my first guest. But I fetched my stuff up last week. I didn't have a lecture until today.'

'Where do you sleep?'

'There's a room across the landing. Last year, I was living in student quarters.'

'What are you studying?'

'Engineering.'

'Not business management?'

Paul Tallis gave him his shy smile. 'Perhaps I've had my nose rubbed in the Press. Just the smell of it turns my stomach – a

72

mixture of printing-ink, glue, hot metal and raw paper, along with a noise level you'd scarcely credit. So I've opted out. My flair is mechanics. For instance, I've always done my own car maintenance. That's my Mini by the gate – souped up, of course: a real bomb.'

'Does engineering stretch to naval architecture?'

'That's another point. I'd love to design yachts.'

'Wasn't your nose rubbed in sailing too?'

His eyes sparkled. 'That's different.'

The kettle boiled and he made the coffee. There wasn't a tray to carry it through on. Gently took charge of the two beakers, Paul Tallis followed with the sugar and a milk-bottle. You couldn't help feeling a student too, in that topsy-turvy room where nothing was in its place: where even to find space to set down two beakers you had to shove aside books, pads, a portable typewriter ...

'Help yourself to milk and sugar.'

Down below, someone was strumming a guitar. Then there were voices raised in laughter, a sound of feet on the lower stairs.

'So what have you really come about, sir?'

He was back on the desk, Gently on the chair. The coffee was sweet if nothing else, and Gently's pipe was drawing comfortably.

'As I said, routine details. We talk to everyone who might be useful. You, because you called at The Uplands on Saturday. Did you deliver a letter, by the way?'

He didn't as much tense as go still.

'I didn't deliver any letter.'

'Think. Weren't you given a note for someone?'

'No – you're absolutely wrong!'

'How am I wrong?'

He had been going to drink, but now he put the beaker down beside him. Gently continued to smoke agreeably, the smoke rising at slow intervals.

'You're talking about the letter they found on him, aren't you?'

'Am I?'

'That's the only letter that interests you. But I didn't take it. In fact –'

'Yes?'

Paul Tallis jerked away, a faint flush in his cheek.

'What time were you there?'

'About eleven.'

'Who did you speak to at The Uplands?'

'Fiona. Auntie Ruth. I believe Uncle Fred was down the garden.'

'But principally Miss Fiona?'

'I wanted her to come with me to Portman Road. But she'd fixed up something with mother, and anyway she didn't want to watch the football.'

'How long were you talking to her?'

'About twenty minutes.'

'You were alone with her?'

He nodded.

'And you didn't give her a letter –'

'No!'

'But perhaps you did see one in her possession?'

Now the faint flush had become a stain. 'Look here! I'm saying nothing to implicate Fiona. I don't know how it all came about, but I'm certain of one thing, she's completely innocent.'

Gently puffed. 'Then you did see her with one.'

'It could have been anything at all.'

'Can you describe it?'

'Just an ordinary envelope.'

'With writing on it?'

His head sank. 'No.'

'Drink your coffee.'

Mechanically, Paul Tallis picked up his beaker and drank. The flush in his face was hot and he kept his eyes well away from Gently's.

'I feel like a traitor.'

Gently hunched. 'You want her father's killer found, don't you?'

'Yes – especially if he's dragged Fiona into it.'

'For that, I'm asking you these questions.'

'So what else can I tell you?'

Gently trailed smoke. 'Where did you go when you left The Uplands?'

Paul Tallis drank more coffee, his hot face set in a resentful expression.

'Are you trying to infer …?'

'I'm inferring nothing. Simply asking for information.'

'I think you tricked me into telling you about the letter. And it needn't have been what you think, at all.'

'Then where did you go?'

'You know where I went!' He was trying to work up indignation. 'It's got nothing to do with it. If you're like this with me, I hate to think how you'll treat Fiona.'

'Didn't you drive to Ipswich?'

'Suppose I did.'

'At what time did you pass by the gorse circle?'

'How would I know? Around half-past eleven.'

'I was going to ask if you noticed anyone about there.'

For a while Paul Tallis stared at the floor, mouth small, eyes scowling; then he took a deep breath and managed a crooked sort of smile.

'I'm sorry! But it's the way it gets me. I'm worried stiff about Fiona.'

'We're not trying to harass her, you know.'

'But put yourself in my position. It seems to me you're trying to get at her – and Uncle Ray too, for the matter of that. As though you suspected some collusion between them, something to do with Uncle Fred's death. It's a bit of a shock, really. I never guessed you'd have suspicions like that.'

Gently inclined his head. 'Perhaps I haven't.'

'Then why are you asking me all these questions?'

'It's just a job, like other jobs.'

Paul Tallis shook his head and drank coffee.

'Anyway, I didn't see anyone. At least, as far as I can remember.'

'A parked vehicle? Perhaps ... a bicycle?'

'You see, I was simply driving without thinking.'

'I expect your mind would have been on the match.'

'Yes, actually.' He sounded surprised. 'Manchester United is always an occasion, there's usually a record crowd for that.'

'Parking problems,' Gently smiled.

'Unless you know the ropes.' Paul Tallis looked arch. 'I was rather naughty. I parked at the station in one of the slots reserved for season-ticket holders. Well, nobody uses them on a Saturday, and the station is handy for Portman Road ... and you can get a ploughman's lunch at the pub across the road.' He checked, flushing. 'Are you a fan?'

Gently shrugged. 'A good match, was it?'

'Yes, a cracker – two-nil. Mariner sewed it up with a glancing header.'

'I'd like to have seen that early goal of Wark's.'

'That too.' Paul Tallis hesitated. 'But why are we talking football?'

Gently grinned wryly. 'Why not? What time did you arrive back?'

'Oh ... I see! What you want to know is whether I saw anything driving home. Well, I didn't.'

'Still, when did you get there?'

'I suppose it would have been half-past six.'

He still seemed a little uncertain, sitting slanted on the desk, beaker forgotten in his hand. Gently's smoke was filling the small room, of which neither of the two modest windows was open. Below the guitar-player had ceased to strum and instead one heard a drone of conversation. The silence in the room had suddenly become awkward, the clutter in it forlorn.

'Look, there is something I must put to you – it's part of my job too.'

'Anything I can tell you ...'

'I want you to reconsider what you told me about delivering a letter to The Uplands.'

'But I've told you the truth –!'

'Listen, this is what I'm asking in so many words. Did your uncle give you the letter to give to Miss Fiona, with certain instructions about what to do with it?'

'As though I'd do such a thing for Uncle Ray ...!'

'But if your mother had asked you, wouldn't you have done it?'

He was up off the desk instantly. 'You just leave my mother out of it!'

There was a fierceness in the blue eyes now and a slight quivering of the lips. Yet, finding the beaker in his hand a little ridiculous, he couldn't help reaching out to set it down. Then he became even more self-conscious: his eyes dropped before Gently's gaze.

'All right then – it's part of your job ... you have to give people jolts like that! Only it's all nonsense, and you know it. Uncle Ray would do his own dirty work.'

'He's capable of it?'

'Perhaps.'

'That isn't quite the impression you were giving earlier.'

'Oh well ... he's family, isn't he? You can't let the side down in things like this.'

Gently's pipe had gone out; he relit it. Paul Tallis stood helplessly by the desk: he seemed to be waiting for some fresh onslaught. But in the end Gently merely rose.

'That's that, then.'

'You've finished with me?'

'Unless you've anything else to tell me.'

Paul Tallis said bitterly: 'There can't be much left to tell you. One way or the other, you'd have had it out of me.'

Smiling, Gently said: 'Just some of the loose ends ...'

He dropped his spent matches in a litter-stuffed bin. They went out to the landing. Strangely, Paul Tallis seemed half-reluctant to let him go.

'Are you coming here again ...?'

'It shouldn't be necessary.'

'I didn't mind you asking the questions. Really.'

'Just as well!'

'Look ... I'm worried. Fiona ... But you do understand, don't you?'

Down below Gently paused on the pavement to appraise the Mini parked there. In metallic blue, it had a spoiler and wide wheels and a fish-tail exhaust that gleamed in the street-light. Psychedelic transfers decorated the body and there was a name: The Time Machine.

Up in the high window, under the eaves, Paul Tallis's face appeared, watching.

7

The moon, now higher and whiter, rode on his right as he drove back, and smoky mist, lying low on fields, here and there leaked across the road. Nevertheless he drove fast. Behind all the calculations of the day had nagged one thought: his phone call in the evening, that precious renewal of broken contact. Already it was late: in France, an hour behind, Gabrielle and Andrée would be thinking of bed; Gabrielle with her ear cocked for the phone, wondering, perhaps beginning to be anxious. And what would he tell her? Should he mention the house? But he knew he would never dare touch on that! At odd moments, since the visit to Welbourne, he'd been fingering his dream, and each time had thrust it aside as impossible. The house was too far out ... except at weekends and on leaves it would have to stay empty and shut up, still a dream, while, at Lime Walk, their real existence would continue and revolve. And yet ... it was already as though his viewpoint were shifting, with London distanced to weekday necessity and his centre of gravity suddenly placed here. Would she want it too? She'd admire the house, but ...? In his mind he decided that, yes, he would perhaps mention it, while ruthlessly avoiding the smallest suggestion ...

Guiltily he checked his speed, aware with a jolt that he had let it race with his thoughts. Seventy-five! Any lurking patrol would have pulled him up and given him a breath-test. At Stansgate he forced himself to a crawl through the cramped vagaries of the one-way, and found himself passing a long, drab, unlit building that extended the whole length of one narrow street. The Tallis Press. He eyed it distastefully, its Victorian brick and stodgy windows, the gaping gateway with stencilled sign: Loading Bay Straight Ahead. Seven hundred jobs and the boss's Rolls: but to him merely the facet of a passing conundrum. Reality was the scent of heather and a phone waiting to ring in far-off Mont St-Aignan ...

And in the end it was almost a frost, that call he'd been waiting all day to make. He'd had to take it at The Gull's reception counter, with the manager making up accounts at his elbow. Then it had to go through International Exchange, meaning a delay of twenty-five minutes; and meanwhile, it seemed, the entire staff of The Gull had chosen that moment to hang around for a gossip.

'You are not alone, my friend ...?'

Scarcely! At the other end it must have sounded like Babel.

'Then I will say it for you. I love you, my friend, and already I am yearning for your arms.'

'Gabrielle ...'

'Yes ...?'

But even in French he couldn't bring himself to say it.

'Sleep well ...'

He heard her little chuckle. 'Perhaps we have better luck next time, hah?'

Grumpily he pushed through into a bar smoky and noisy at the end of the evening, ordered a pint and sandwich and squatted with them on a bar-stool. A contact so short, so precious! Ridiculous to think of mentioning the house. It was just hearing each other, a moment of illusion, a trying-to-believe that, if one reached out ...

In the noise and laughter he gulped his beer and bolted the sandwich in chunks.

'You look a bit down in the mouth, old lad.'

Turning, he found Reymerston standing beside him. The painter was regarding him with a half-smile, an empty glass in his hand. He reached for Gently's glass.

'Fill them up, Sid.'

He didn't take his eyes from Gently's. As always with Reymerston, you felt immediate rapport, a sensation of sympathetic understanding.

'I take it your sums aren't coming right yet.'

Gently grunted: 'I may have been handed the wrong sums!'

'Naughty,' Reymerston smiled. 'But don't take it to heart. You can always fall back on me if you have to.'

'Do you really mean that?'

'I'm still the leading contender. And I hear you were down Archie's well today.'

His eyes twinkled. If he were fishing, there was nothing in his attitude to indicate it; just the amused, relaxed buoyancy that was the trademark of the man. How could one suspect him? Stack the facts how you would, and still they fell down when you looked him in the eye ...

He paid for the drinks and raised his glass.

'I called in at Ruth's earlier this evening. She was impressed, you know. Both by what you asked her and what you didn't. Cried a bit, but not too much.' He touched his glass to Gently's. 'Cheers.'

'So what do you two plan now?'

Reymerston laughed. 'That's a leading question. But I'll take it in all innocence. When she says Yes, I plan to marry her.'

'Hasn't she said it?'

'Is that a mark against me? Naturally, I haven't asked her yet. But unless you clap me in jail I shall ask her – once this business has been cleared up. So here's to detection.' He drank. 'Dare I ask how it's coming along?'

Perhaps only Reymerston, in such circumstances, would have asked that question outright. Gently drank too.

'I've just rung my wife.'

'No problems at home?' Reymerston asked.

'No problems. But she's in France, so I had to make the call from the desk.'

'Scarcely *entre nous*,' Reymerston smiled. 'But you're welcome to use my phone if you like. Will she often be in France?'

'She has a business there.'

Reymerston nodded and drank.

Yet wasn't it preposterous to be chatting like this with a man who remained the principal suspect? As though somehow his guilt or innocence belonged to a different order of things? Gently hunched over his glass. Beside them last orders were being called. If he could have made that call again, alone, in a silence far removed ...

'Is the moon up, old lad?'

'The moon ...?'

'We could take a stroll along the beach.'

Gently stared at him 'Why do that?'

Reymerston smiled back. 'Just a thought. You seem in need of someone to talk to.'

The devil take him! Yet it was true: he felt a need to wind down with someone. And Reymerston ... why not? If he kept his wits about him ...

'All right.'

They drank up together and set down glasses side by side.

'The truth is,' Reymerston said, 'I'm in much the same boat. I couldn't get my woman alone, either.'

The moon was up: bright and clear it shone on house-front and gable, lighting the way to a low lane that led by a flood wall to the sand dunes. They pushed by tamarisk and bramble and passed a line of silent beach huts; then below spread the beach and the shimmering flakes of combers.

All was plain in the cold light: northward, the jet-like piles of the jetty; southward, the outward sweep of the bay, stretching afar, with a shadow of cliffs. Rashes of shingle divided the beach between the soft sand and the firm; wash spread over the latter, leaving dark stains of seaweed.

The air was cool but not chill; the rustle of surf made a continuous rumble.

'Almost unpaintable,' Reymerston said, as they reached the firm going and set off along the tideline. 'Heaven knows I've tried, and Crome before me, but all we've done is make pictures. Perhaps you can't paint moonlight, or not on the sea. There doesn't seem the right sort of paint on the palette.'

'Perhaps you should leave it to the likes of Debussy.'

'Debussy saw it through cellophane,' Reymerston said. 'He was making pictures too. But then you walk down here, smell the seaweed, and despair. Art has limits. All you can do is pick your spot and try to reach it.'

'This afternoon I spoke to one of your patrons.'

'Sarah Jonson,' Reymerston said. 'She rang me.' He strode on silently for a space. 'What did you think of her house?'

'I'd like to buy it. But I daren't.'

'You'd be an idiot not to if it suits. Heatherings is special. You could search the county and never find another like it.' He paused again. 'It would suit you better than Tallis.'

'Sarah Jonson talks too much,' Gently said.

'Not too much,' Reymerston said. 'Just a mention of why you were there. I may have led her on. And Tallis was late.'

'People sometimes are late,' Gently said.

'*Touché*,' Reymerston smiled. 'But I was waiting to emerge from Hare Lane when he passed up the street. At around one forty-five.'

Gently didn't reply. They kept walking over the flat, crunchy sand, the moon's path on their left dredging flashes from the sea. Very far out a tiny mist of light marked a position on the horizon: a vessel, hull-down. Like the moon, she went with them.

'This evening, I talked to Paul Tallis.'

Reymerston let a few strides go by. Then he said: 'Paul's a likeable youngster. And, of course, he's thick with Fiona Quennell.'

'I found him puzzling.'

'Puzzling ...?'

'I couldn't make up my mind about him. Whether he was naïve or rather clever. At times he seemed both.'

'Probably naïve,' Reymerston said. 'But I think I know what you mean. Paul has had to face up to a few things and sometimes he strikes you as a bit withdrawn. A pity, because he has a nice nature. Ruth is very fond of Paul.'

'At home, he lives in the Tallis cottage.'

'Yes.' Reymerston let it lie.

'Apparently, out of deference to the newly-married couple.'

Again Reymerston took strides before replying.

'You want to know if you can trust him, don't you?'

'What are his relations with his stepfather?'

Reymerston shrugged. 'I've never seen them together, but according to Ruth, pretty rugged. He only visits the house in his stepfather's absence and otherwise cuts him when they meet. That's hearsay, agreed. But perhaps you shouldn't trust any allegations he makes against his stepfather.'

'Or the reverse?'

'The reverse ...?'

'When he sets out to defend his stepfather?'

Reymerston shook his head. 'If that's the case, I can well imagine you being puzzled! May I know from what?'

He stared closely at Gently, his face gaunt under the moon. Gently said nothing. Walking on the inshore side, he had his face in shadow.

'Are you thinking Paul is tied up in this?'

'Perhaps Paul. Perhaps Fiona Quennell.'

'Not Fiona,' Reymerston said definitely. 'Paul if you like, but not Fiona. That's too *outré*. Fiona wouldn't. But if it comes to that, why would Paul?'

'Did Fiona know about you and her mother?'

'Not till now, as far as I know.'

'She is apparently unstable.'

Reymerston kept staring, feet crunching ahead through small shingle. At last he turned away.

'No. You're backing the wrong horse, old lad.'

'She loves her mother ...'

Reymerston's reply was a simple toss of the head.

They had come half a mile or more, with the darkness of cliffs drawing sensibly closer. The soft rumble of surf, by repetition, had reduced itself to an unregarded accompaniment. The sound was isolating: they walked contained in it, along the moon-drawn line between sea and shore. Breaking foam seemed more solid in the moonlight, a hesitating sculpture in silver-white.

Reymerston said: 'Do you know this coast?'

'I've had other cases this way,' Gently said.

'Will your wife like it?'

'She comes from Normandy.'

'Ah,' Reymerston said. 'Then she'll like it.'

'Do you know Normandy?'

'I'm a painter.'

'She comes from Rouen.'

'I know Rouen. What's her name?'

'Gabrielle.'

'Gabrielle,' Reymerston repeated.

Before them stretched an encroachment of the sea that would have called for a detour.

'This will do, I think,' Reymerston said. 'Let's sit a moment in the sandhills.'

They crossed shingle and soft sand of the beach and climbed the low dunes. Behind them lay salt marsh with a heavy dark of distant trees. From up there the moon's path reached longer and the broken line of surf extended south to an infinity. A light breeze blew on the tops, warm, and sufficient to stir the marrams.

They found a bank of sand and sat. Reymerston picked up a fat pebble to toy with. Then he pitched it at the beach, where it landed on shingle with a ringing sound.

'Have you talked to Tallis, old lad?'

Gently gazed at the sea and said nothing.

'What did you make of him?' Reymerston asked.

Gently went on watching the sea.

Reymerston laughed. 'You won't tell me, so let me put the case to you. You're stuck between us, him and me. Because we've both got the same things going for us. Isn't that true?'

Still Gently said nothing.

'My side we know about,' Reymerston said. 'So let's talk about Tallis. I know, and probably you know, that he left home with plenty of time in hand. Yet he was nearly an hour late at Heatherings, leaving a gap which you'd want him to explain. And he did explain it, only my guess is that his explanation explained nothing.' He glanced at Gently. 'Any comment?'

Gently jammed an empty pipe in his mouth.

'Taken as read, then,' Reymerston smiled. 'Like me, Tallis doesn't have an alibi. Now we come to motive, and I would be surprised if you hadn't faced him with that. He has it in handfuls. He was over a barrel after what happened on *Spindrift*. Exactly how far over a barrel only he knows, but it was evidently enough. So how would he play it? By protesting his unfailingly cordial relations with Freddy Quennell, and by representing his promotion as an astute piece of business. And you, of course, stony-faced, took it all for what it was worth: not very much. And so, like me, Raymond Tallis has a fat motive.'

Gently sucked air through his pipe, but didn't otherwise interrupt his meditation. Reymerston felt for another pebble; he juggled it between his hands.

'Next, the letter. Allow it is the forgery which I, of course, know it to be. How did it get to Freddy Quennell? Well, you've been talking to friend Paul. Paul was at The Uplands on Saturday morning, Ruth remembered that; and now you're interested to know the precise relations between Paul and his stepfather. Not much doubt about what you're thinking: that Paul worked the letter off on Quennell – with or without Fiona's connivance, though innocently, we agree. Now he's standing by his stepfather, while poor Fiona is in shock; but that's how Freddy Quennell got the letter that sent him on his merry way.' Reymerston grinned ruefully. 'Or, alternatively, the letter originated with Ruth and me.'

Unmoved, Gently sucked his pipe. Reymerston tossed the pebble and caught it.

'No proof – that's your real problem. Nothing solid either on Tallis or me. You have to believe it of one or other of us, but there are difficulties either way. Tallis gives explanations you can't check while I simply stick with a plea of innocence. But the letter got left on the body, and I have a track record for disposing of evidence.' He tossed the pebble. 'And now, old lad, you sit here letting me talk my head off, hoping no doubt I shall drop a clanger that will put my guileless shoulder into your clutches.'

He threw the pebble; this time it landed with a thump in soft sand; then he, too, pulled out a pipe and stuck it empty in his mouth. Now two faint smudges of light were moving imperceptibly at the sea's rim, while, from the direction of town, one could catch the red stare of the Wolmering Light.

'What tobacco do you smoke ...?'

'Here.'

Reymerston tossed him his pouch. It contained a Scotch mixture, cut broad and with a fair proportion of latakia. They filled and lit; Reymerston lay back against the marrams. Below them, the moonlit surf had a frolic appearance, almost animal.

'You know ... I'm getting weary of tragedy.' The red blinks from the light were catching Reymerston's face. 'One way or another, it seems to have followed me all my life.'

'You mean what happened over there,' Gently said.

'No, before that. A couple of years earlier it was my wife.' His mouth twitched. 'She had a lover who she used to visit when I was absent on business. I knew, and I didn't care. She thought she had pulled the wool over my eyes. Every time I arrived home she took care to be there before me. Then one night she was late and probably driving like a lunatic. She overtook a line of cars and got squeezed between the last of them and a truck.'

Loosing smoke, Gently said: 'Yet you made it pay off.'

Reymerston stared, then shook his head. 'In an ironic sort of way, I suppose you could call me a lucky man! Linda died, and it gave me perfect cover for my resignation and disappearance. They saw me as a broken man. But my plans had been made long before.'

'To you, her death was no tragedy.'

'All such deaths are a tragedy,' Reymerston insisted. 'I didn't hate Linda, I wished her well. For ten years her life was mingled with mine. Her dying was atrocious. My grief wasn't acted. Simply, she wasn't the right woman for me.'

'And since then you have lived alone.'

He nodded. 'For that reason, partly. But partly because alone was what I needed to be. I had to come to terms with myself, and anyone else would have got in the way.' He sighed suddenly. 'But partly that. In the long run, it's people who count. Like it or not, you belong to them and bleed when they're torn away.'

He brooded for a time over his pipe.

'Then that Selly woman found me. A pitiful, futile creature who came homing in like an act of doom. Yet – why to me? If she had wanted to end it, she had only to walk down the beach.'

'Your luck again,' Gently said.

'My luck.' He took a number of quick puffs. 'You know, all I can feel about her is a sort of bewildered anger.'

'Against her?'

'Not against her. Probably more against myself. That I was overcome and did what I did, I swear without consciously sinister intent. If I had known that night what I've learned since I would have given the poor wench some money. I wept when I left her out there. The futility of it stunned me.'

'Yet you disposed of the evidence.'

'Why not. I felt more sinned against than sinning.'

'Have you told Mrs Quennell?'

Reymerston sank his head. 'Not yet. But I shall have to.'

He sucked defiantly on his pipe. Gently continued to smoke placidly. Only a few of the bright stars were visible behind the brilliance of the moon. The breeze shaking the marrams made a papery sound, oddly suggesting the noise of insects; it brought with it the warm, musky smell of sere vegetation.

'Marion couldn't take it. You remember Marion?'

'Marion ...'

She had been the headmistress of Huntingfield School. And suddenly, surprisedly, Gently did remember her: then realised why he had suppressed the memory. She'd resembled Gabrielle. A little older, but a similar cast of feature and sturdy figure, the same firmness of speech and manner. She and Reymerston had had a liaison.

'You confessed to her?'

'I felt I had to. She was so cut up about the Rede girl. I was to blame. I should have owned up earlier. Marion could never forgive me for that.'

'You didn't know the Rede girl would behave so foolishly.'

'But if I'd gone to you earlier she'd have been under no pressure. Yet if I had done, would you have believed me?'

Gently puffed. Most probably he wouldn't!

'She had met Vivienne.'

'I know.'

Marion Swefling had taken prompt action. After learning of sex orgies involving three pupils, she had gone to have it out with Vivienne Selly. And that had been the last blow, for Vivienne. She had made a pitiful attempt to seduce Marion Swefling. Then she had reached the end, broken, isolated: it could have been the sea, but she chose Reymerston.

'Marion handled her better than I did.'

'Miss Swefling was responsible for what happened after.'

'Marion was ...?'

Gently nodded to the stars. Yes, looking back, that must have been the critical moment. Shocked and disgusted by Vivienne's behaviour, Marion Swefling had hastened from the cottage. She had been too insensitive: hadn't realised the bitter need of the other woman. She represented the pride, the standing of the successful world to which Vivienne had appealed for so long, and so hopelessly. Contemptuously, she had rejected Vivienne Selly. And Vivienne could take no more.

'Vivienne tried to make love to her.'

'She told me.'

'How would you expect her to react to that?'

'In her profession, Marion Swefling had experience in handling emotional females.'

'You didn't know Vivienne.'

'Because I got to know her I had to believe what you told me. But Marion Swefling was guilty too. If it's any consolation, she was your accomplice.'

Reymerston was silent.

'What happened to her?'

'She took another post, up in Yorkshire. But we'd broken up long before that. It was about then that I crossed the river.'

He rose, stretched and knocked out his pipe. Now the moon was dulling over with some wisps of wrack. For a moment Reymerston stared again at the winking town lights, then dropped his eyes to the still-seated Gently.

'Have you settled about me yet?'

Gently looked up at him. 'Along with me, you have to convince Eyke.'

'If Ruth is innocent, wouldn't I be?'

'Mrs Quennell doesn't know what we know.'

'That once I killed ...'

He stood silent for a time, a downcast figure against the sea. At last he shrugged, rather pettishly.

'Come on ... I'm for bed!'

So they walked back over the tops, going single file through the sandy gaps. At The Gull they parted; in the park before it, Gently's Princess was the only car.

8

Nevertheless it was a long time before he got to sleep that night. His bed was too soft, and the moaning of the surf, though distant, kept him wakeful. At Lime Walk it had been the traffic, which at Finchley he'd long ceased to notice; not because the sound had been louder at Lime Walk, but simply because it was different. Here there were no sounds at all except that vigilant, monotonous scouring. And somehow it sounded threatening, as though it were merely biding its time.

He slept at last, to wake with a throbbing head and foul mouth. But now the sun was out of the sea and the latter scaled with flashing light. He peered at it heavy-eyed for a while before collecting his toilet bag and shuffling off to the bathroom. He'd only had a couple of pints ... had they come from the lees of the barrel?

Because he was about so early they weren't ready for him down below, and it was half an hour before the solitary waitress began to furbish his table for breakfast. He was midway through the meal when he heard a car park: Eyke. The local Inspector came in briskly, a gleam in his usually cautious eye.

'Sir, I think we're on to something!'

'Sit down, and pour yourself some coffee.'

'Sir, this could be important ...'

Gently nodded to the waitress, who lounged at the hatch a short distance away.

'Miss, another cup.'

Eyke sat down, but clearly he was holding himself in with difficulty. He gulped his coffee, and watched impatiently while Gently spread honey on a second piece of toast. But the waitress continued to hover, and Gently to avoid his eye. Finally, it was in the empty lounge that Gently stuck his pipe in his mouth and said:

'Now!'

'It's the lab boys, sir. They were out early this morning at the scene.'

'Looking for what?'

'They'd got a theory, sir, which they wanted to check out. They were a bit narked because we were chasing them and they tried what you said with a lump of horse-meat. That gave them a bright idea, and they wanted to check if it was on.'

'And what was the bright idea?'

'That Quennell was shot with an arrow, sir, by a chummie concealed in that hollow bush.'

'An arrow ...!'

'Yes, sir, a sharpened arrow, probably one with a metal tip. I met them out there just now, and they're pretty certain that's what happened. As Quennell walked past the bush, chummie let fly into his back.'

Gently dragged hard on his pipe. An arrow ... was it credible? It would certainly answer all the queries, about both the weapon and the scene. The latter especially: it had gone on bothering him how chummie had successfully approached his victim, soundlessly emerging and stalking him until in a position to strike the blow. But waiting in the bush with a drawn bow ... that was an answer to every objection. And through the gap cut in the bush, hadn't he seen Eyke's back come into view when Eyke had been precisely at the spot where Quennell had fallen?

'Is there a local archery club?'

'Yes, sir.' Perhaps one could forgive Eyke's note of complacency! 'I know the secretary, sir, Dick Barham, and I rang him before I came here. According to him the membership is mostly from Ipswich, and offhand he knew of nobody who lives in the village. But they shoot in the forest near Grimchurch. Colonel Jonson, sir – he was a member.'

'Never mind Colonel Jonson! Has Barham a list?'

'Yes, sir. He's checking it for me.'

'Ring him again.'

'I gave him this number, sir. Unfortunately, he keeps the records at his office.'

A stupid delay. Fretfully, Gently threw himself down on one of the lounge's orange-seated chairs. In the list in that idiot's office might be the single, the vital entry. Suddenly, they'd got a lead that could point in a definite and unequivocal direction – given half a grain of luck. In minutes they could know which way it was to go ...

'Where is Barham's office?'

'In Stansgate, sir. He should be there by now.'

Probably reading his mail or chatting to his secretary: anything but getting out that list.

Chewing on the pipe, Gently stared at the paintings that crowded the lounge walls, each ticketed with a price and the name of some hopeful dauber.

'Sir, did you speak to Paul Tallis?'

'I didn't think to ask him if he was an archer!'

'Well ... no, sir. What I was wondering was how much he knew about his uncle.'

It was a fair question. Mastering his impatience, Gently gave Eyke a synopsis of his visit, of the ambivalent impression he had received, his conclusion that Paul Tallis knew more than he was saying. Eyke listened blank-faced.

'So like that, sir, his uncle had cause to be a bit worried.'

'That's how it looks. Paul Tallis knows plenty, but he's making believe to stand by his uncle.'

'Making believe, sir?'

Gently hesitated. 'That's the impression I finally came away with. That young Paul was protesting a little too much and wasn't averse to my suspecting his uncle. By his account there's no ill-feeling. He was ready to excuse his uncle for everything. But he took care to bring out the case against him and to let me think that Miss Quennell knows some more about the yachting tragedy.'

'That could be true, sir. Quennell may have talked about it at home.'

'In that case Frank Quennell would know of it. And he would have been the first to throw it at us.'

'Something she heard and he didn't, sir.'

Gently shrugged and sieved smoke.

'You say he saw her with the letter in her hand?'

'Just a letter. According to him.'

'Well, that fits in, sir ...'

'That's the trouble. Young Paul is bright enough to read between the lines.'

He blew smoke towards the paintings.

'Listen. I threw him a trick question. Kick-off at Portman Road was three o'clock, and I'd like to be certain he was there to see it. I've a description of his car, which according to him was parked in the station yard from about half-past twelve. Also he may have had lunch in the pub opposite. See what Ipswich can turn up on that.'

'You're thinking, sir ...?'

'Paul Tallis is a nice lad, but if he's holding something back I want to know it.'

There was stationery on the table: Gently jotted down details. He was still scribbling when the waitress came to summon Eyke to the phone. Five minutes later Eyke returned with his face full of news.

'This has to be it, sir.'

'Get on with it!'

'The Tallis brothers, sir. They were both members. The old man, Walter, was a founder member, and both his sons are listed.'

They stared at each other.

'How long ago was it?'

'Not since 1959, sir. Barham rang a senior member and got some details from him. It seems the Tallises fancied the old lance-wood bows and dropped out when the modern bows came in. But old Walter used to shoot in his garden after that, and likely his sons did too.'

Gently sucked at a dead pipe. 'Can you get a warrant?'

'Yes, sir. Right away.'

'Get it.'

Eyke nodded and hurried back to the phone.

And suddenly a feeling of inevitability, of cards beginning to come off the pack. The more so when they collared Raymond Tallis just about to step into his car.

'I'm afraid we shall need you, Mr Tallis.'

'What –? I'm late for business already –'

'We require your presence.'

And in his shifty eyes a quirk of helpless fear ...

'What's my nephew been saying?'

'Shall we go in?'

You could almost smell the fear on him. With a sort of childish petulance he slammed the door of the Daimler and stumped before them into the house. In the hall they met Julia Tallis, still in a dressing-gown, and her eyes too were big with apprehension.

'What's it about now, Ray –?'

She followed them into the lounge, which smelled shut-up and stale with cigar smoke.

'Listen, I demand to know –'

'Please sit down, Mr Tallis.'

'But I tell you, I'm overdue at the business.'

Nevertheless, he plumped down in a chair.

'Now ... just one or two questions.'

There was certainly fear in that gloomy room!

'I understand you used to be an archer. How long ago since you gave it up?'

'I ... what?'

The creased eyes had sprung open, and the fleshy mouth dropped. He gazed helplessly at Julia Tallis, whose face looked pallid and unwashed.

'Good God, are you suggesting –?'

'Just answer the question, Mr Tallis.'

'Oh no,' Julia Tallis wailed, and she too dropped on to a chair.

'Well?' Gently said.

'This is ... fantastic.'

'Is there archery equipment on the premises?'

'No – yes, there may be! Arthur may have kept his gear. But I can't believe ...' He stared fearfully at Gently. 'Look, you've got to tell me what Paul's been saying! He's capable of inventing any story – ask his mother, if you don't believe me.'

'It's true,' Julia Tallis wailed. 'Paul has never forgiven Ray for marrying me. You mustn't believe him. And Ray hasn't touched a bow since he was a young man, living at home.'

'Have you ever used a bow, Mrs Tallis?'

'I! You can't imagine –'

'But have you?'

'All right, I have! But it was only to please Arthur.'

'So where is your archery equipment kept?'

'Can't you understand? This was years ago – when we were first married, before Paul came. I don't even know if we still have any.'

'But if you had, where would it be?'

'This – this is just unbelievable!' Raymond Tallis broke in. 'I was never even keen on the wretched sport. It was father and Arthur who shot in matches. They dressed up in Lincoln green, pretending they were Robin Hood or something. Then the club opted for the new bow, and father let our membership lapse.'

'But there was shooting after that?'

'Not by me! And father died in '63.'

'Do you mind if we take a look round?'

With a burst of defiance, Raymond Tallis said: 'Just try it!'

'A search warrant is on its way.'

Julia Tallis gave a low moan. She sat with clasped arms: she looked sluttish in the dressing-gown, which gaped to reveal an ample figure. Tallis was breathing a little fast and darting fearful looks at Gently. There was darkness under his eyes, suggesting he hadn't slept too well.

'If you find Arthur's bow, do you mean to arrest me?'

Gently stared but said nothing.

'Look, they were wooden bows, lance-wood bows. If I'd done what you're thinking, wouldn't I have got rid of it?'

'Would you have got rid of it?'

'I'm not stupid!'

'How would you have got rid of a wooden bow?'

'Well – broken it up, burnt it. You wouldn't expect me to bring it back here.'

'You'd have time for that?'

'What? What do you mean?'

Gently didn't tell him what he meant. Raymond Tallis stared with squinting eyes, his yellowish teeth showing.

'I did go down to those moorings, you know. I've put in a written report to the club.'

'You have a witness now?'

'No, I don't! But I dare say someone would have seen me. It's up to you, that, isn't it?'

'Someone who can place you there for an hour?'

'An hour, two hours, what does it matter? I say I was there, now you prove different.' But the idea didn't seem to console him. 'If no one saw me, what are you going to do?'

'Why does what your nephew might say bother you?'

At once the panic button was pressed! Raymond Tallis jerked forward in his chair, hands gripping the stuffed leather arms.

'Is it his idea – this?'

'Which idea, Mr Tallis?'

'You know damned well which idea. That someone laid for Freddy with a bow.'

'Laid for him …?'

'I've seen the place. That's natural, isn't it? I went to see it. And there's a hiding-place there, in the gorse, where someone's cut a piece away. Well, if Freddy was shot with an arrow, ten to one who did it was hiding in there. But yesterday there wasn't any talk of an arrow, so where else would you have got the idea?'

'I believe your nephew was resident here until Sunday.'

'In the cottage – he doesn't live here.'

'Surely that amounts to the same thing?'

'No, it doesn't. He's never in the house while I'm around.'

'Yet ... he was about here?'

'Oh my God. If he's your witness, I'll cut him to ribbons. He blames me for what happened to Arthur, and – and ... who's going to believe him?'

'On Saturday morning he visited The Uplands.'

'You're crazy if you think he took that letter!'

'But, if he were ignorant of the contents ...?'

'Ask yourself, why would he do it for me?'

'But ... for Mrs Tallis?'

Julia Tallis flared: 'Oh, this is stupid, stupid! How can you believe it? That I would use Paul in a – plot against Freddy?'

'Is that your bureau over there, Mrs Tallis?'

'What's it to you if it's my bureau?'

'Shortly a search warrant will be delivered. I was wondering if you would mind if I anticipated it.'

She stared, big-eyed. 'You leave it alone.'

Gently shrugged. 'I'm willing to wait.'

'But this ... this is beyond anything!'

She gazed at her husband. Both of them now were very pale.

'Listen,' Raymond Tallis said. 'I've had enough. I'm going to get my lawyer out here. I'm not going to be bullied into taking the rap – fitted up, isn't that what you call it?'

But he spoke it without conviction, sitting there looking ghastly in the big chair. And Julia Tallis, her blonde hair straggling, continued to stare with hunted eyes.

'This is a nightmare ...'

'Perhaps we can go over your movements again, Mr Tallis.'

'You know my movements!'

'I don't think you told me at what time you left your house on Saturday.'

He hesitated, eyes darting. 'All right, then. It was after two.'

'But you left before your wife.'

'No, that was a mistake. She thought I'd gone, but I hadn't.'

'So a witness who saw you pass up the street at an earlier time would have been in error.'

'A witness?' He gripped the chair-arms. 'Look, you're bullying me till I don't know what I'm saying. The fact is I don't know precisely. My impression is it was after two.'

'If you were seen at one-forty-five ...'

'I'm telling you, then I was still at the house.'

'But you can't remember precisely?'

He dragged on the chair-arms. 'I'm doing my best.'

Evidently.

'Then you drove where?'

Raymond Tallis's pale face set in a sullen expression. 'Listen, I won't go on with this. You're trying to trap me. I'm saying no more till there's a lawyer present.'

'You are free to call one.'

'So then you'll think I'm guilty, wanting a lawyer to hold my hand. I can't win, can I? You've got me both ways. And all on some lies my nephew has told you.'

'Your nephew ...'

Julia Tallis moaned: 'Oh, my son, my son!'

Then suddenly Raymond Tallis's eyes jumped open, staring past Gently to the window. Just as yesterday, Fiona Quennell was standing with her bicycle at the gate.

'Get out ... clear off!'

He sprang to his feet and made violent signs from the window. But for a moment Fiona Quennell stood her ground, gazing at him with her empty eyes. Then she went.

'That crack-brained bitch gets on my nerves – it was her who set Paul against me.'

He shambled to the cabinet and poured whisky.

Julia Tallis said: 'For me too ...'

The warrant came, and along with it two DCs, Bayliss and Hopgood. Gently exhibited the warrant to Tallis, who glared at it helplessly.

'So what happens now?'

'That's up to you. Where do we look for archery equipment?'

'I tell you I don't know if there is any –!'

Julia Tallis said tonelessly: 'Try the attics.'

Eyke dispatched the DCs. Neither Tallis nor his wife made a move to accompany them. He was standing by the marble mantelpiece, nursing more whisky, she remained in her chair, a woebegone figure.

'You want to look through my bureau.'

'With your permission.'

'Damn you, there are personal things in there! Arthur's old letters and things like that. I don't want your grubby fingers among them.'

'We shall take great care.'

'What's that got to do with it? I can tell you there's nothing there for you. Isn't it enough that you're going through the house, without prying into my personal affairs?'

'I regret that I must insist.'

'And if I don't let you?'

'I still have authority to proceed.'

She stared hate at him. Gently's face was blank. He and Eyke approached the bureau. The flap was unlocked; it let down to reveal stuffed slots and boxed stationery. Eyke pointed to the brand: white Basildon Bond, some with printed address, some plain. Also envelopes. And in a slot, picture-postcards of La Baule, bearing Ruth Quennell's handwriting. Then the blotter:

'Look here, sir ...'

The top sheet was almost virgin. There was however a faint squiggle near one of the lower corners. They pored over it. The blotted hand resembled that on the postcards. With difficulty one could make it out to read: 'namoW d'.

'Sir ... the signature.'

In a corner of the bureau stood a bottle of blue Quink ; but the only writing implements with it were a collection of ball pens. Gently turned to Julia Tallis.

'If I may, I would like to see your handbag.'

'But that's beyond everything –!'

'The Inspector will go with you to fetch it.'

'Listen –' Tallis began, but catching Gently's eye shut up and hunched over his glass.

Furiously Julia Tallis stalked out, trailing behind her the embarrassed Eyke; they could hear her angry voice from somewhere above and, when they returned, Eyke's face was pink.

'There.'

'Turn it out, if you will.'

She up-ended the handbag on a table. Out streamed a collection of notes, loose change, keys, papers, cosmetics; and a Waterman pen. Gently took the latter, uncapped it and made a stroke on the blotter. The hue matched the squiggle. He recapped the pen and placed it with the other exhibits.

'I regret that I must take charge of these items. You will of course be issued with a receipt.'

'And I can't stop you, can I?'

'They will be returned if we do not require them.'

Her eyes were large with anger and fear. 'You think I wrote that letter, don't you. Well, I didn't – and I don't care what you've found. Besides, that bureau is never locked up.'

'Your pen is usually kept in your handbag?'

'That's just where you're wrong, it's usually in there! But yesterday I had to write a cheque, and that's the only reason it was in my handbag. So anybody could have used it.'

'Who, Mrs Tallis?'

'Anybody – I don't know! People come here.' Her eyes went suddenly still. 'Fiona. Fiona treats the house as though it were her own.'

'Miss Quennell ...?'

'Yes – Fiona. One day last week she was here by herself. Paul was in Norwich, and I was dressing. She'd have plenty of time to do it.'

'But why would she, Mrs Tallis?'

'Why? Who knows what goes on in her mind?'

'You are suggesting she would plot against her father?'

'She could have written that letter, that's all I know.'

For a moment her stare held, trying to compel him with her conviction. Then her face crumpled.

'Oh my God ... Ray is right. It's all a nightmare!'

The two DCs returned.

'Afraid we've drawn a blank up there, sir.'

'Fetch a bag for this stuff.'

One of them went out to the cars to fetch a bag.

Gently scribbled a receipt. Then he took a sheet of the stationery, folded it, sealed it in an envelope and put it in his pocket. He handed the receipt to Tallis.

'Where else shall we look?'

Tallis's fearful eyes were watering. The glass he hung on to was at least his third, each one filled to near the brim.

'What does it matter ... now? I mean, if you find it, or if you don't! Both ways you've got me. I haven't a leg ... unless someone comes forward who saw me ...'

'Have you anything to tell me?'

'What's the use of that? One day I knew Paul would try to get even. And him you'll believe, not me. Him and that cocky young Quennell ...'

'The cottage has been vacant since Sunday.'

'Do you think I'd hide anything in there!'

'I'll take the key.'

'Go on, have the lot. There's a loft to the garage ... you mustn't miss that.'

With a shaking hand he passed over his keys, among which were those of the plum-coloured Daimler. Meanwhile the DCs had packed the items taken from the bureau in a plastic bag.

They left Tallis to his whisky, his wife to her sobs.

'Right ... first we'll check the car and garage. And one of you search the garden for evidence of a recent bonfire.'

Bayliss set out down the garden, Hopwood took the keys of the car. Another key let them into the garage, in which stood a Lancia, doubtless Julia Tallis's. At one end a bench was surrounded by clutter, but most you could take in at a glance: Eyke set a pile of worn tyres rolling, to reveal only a cobwebbed corner.

'The loft, then ...'

Wooden stairs led to it. It contained the lumber of numerous decades – furniture, boxes, rolls of carpet, even the rusted frame of a motorbike.

'Hold up, sir, someone's been this way.'

The planked floor was floury with dust. A trail led through it, dodging in and out of the lumber, towards the far end of the loft.

'No clear footprints.'

'Chummie came and went, sir.'

'So let's see where he leads us.'

They followed the trail down the loft to a heap in a corner, covered by an old curtain.

'He trod around a bit here, sir.'

'Off with that curtain ...'

For a moment all they could see was dusty crockery and piles of books. Then, in shadows at the back, the patched round face of an old straw target ...

'This is it, sir!'

'Careful ...'

What they really needed was a light: the loft was lit only by a couple of cobwebbed panes, set one each side at the roof's centre. Gently struck a match. Beside the target, fluffy with dust, lay a folded tripod; also, half-hidden behind the target, a leather quiver containing arrows. His match went out: he struck another, bending closer over the stacked crockery. In dust alongside the folded tripod lay a ghostly outline: as of a bow.

'Get a photographer and dabs men out here.'

'Yes, sir.' Eyke was almost holding his breath.

Gingerly, Gently leaned forward and withdrew an arrow from the quiver. About a metre long, in lightweight wood, its varnish finish chafed and bruised: at one end flighted with goose-feather, at the other tipped with a blunt brass tip.

'What we didn't find down the well ...'

'He would need to have sharpened it up a bit, sir.'

'Plenty of files down below.'

They stared at each other, then headed for the trap-door.

And down below you spotted it at once: yellow filings speckling the hinge of a vice, others scattered on the bench-top adjacent, yet more on the concrete floor below. On the tool rack above, an assortment of files: including a six-inch flat with yellowed teeth.

Eyke took it down and turned it to the light.

'I reckon this about sews it up, sir.'

'Have the filings collected and sent to the lab along with the file, an arrow and the other stuff.'

'Yes, sir.'

'We want the brass matched, the paper, the ink, the blotter impression. Also expert opinion on the match of writing and nib.'

'Yes, sir.'

'And any dabs going on the handle of that file and the handle of the vice.'

They were interrupted by the entry of Bayliss.

'Sir, the garden incinerator was used recently. There's a pile of dry ash under it, mostly wood ash and charred paper.'

Gently nodded to the wall, where a sieve was hanging.

'Sift every last pinch of it.'

9

At which point, as though in obedience to a law as yet unformulated by Professor Parkinson, three press cars arrived and impudently drove in at the gate. Reporters and cameramen piled out, the latter at once going into action: clicking at Gently, the police cars and the house, from a window in which a face hastily vanished. Wrathfully Gently strode among them.

'Clear out of this, the whole pack of you.'

'Now, Chiefie, don't be like that ...'

'Take your cars and get back on the road.'

But clearly they weren't going to be satisfied with a brush-off, though they reluctantly shifted the cars. The cameras went on clicking and cassette recorders were held at the ready.

'There'll be a statement later – at the station.'

'Chiefie, the weapon –'

'Never mind the weapon.'

'A little bird says Quennell had Tallis in a bind –'

'Don't tell me, tell your editor.'

'Chiefie, it's a matter of record –'

'So print the record, and blow.'

'Now Chiefie, we have to live too!'

'Some other time – but not here.'

At last he drew a long breath.

'So get your little boxes switched on.'

Instantly a battery of them were thrust towards him, while lofted cameras clicked overhead.

'Local people are assisting the police in tracing the movements of the dead man Quennell. Progress is being made but the weapon has not yet been found. Yesterday the police inspected a well in a village property, but this is not now thought to have a connection with the crime.'

'Chiefie, what well!' came from all over.

'A well to which our attention had been drawn.'

'Now Chiefie, gives us a break ...!'

'That's all for now – and the charge is obstruction if you come back through that gate.'

Muttering, they drew off to the cars, there to hold a huddled conference; then, leaving two scouts, they drove away towards the village, doubtless to start the quest for Archie's well ...

A comic interlude – but the grey face reappearing in the window was not amused. With dead eyes Tallis stared at the two reporters still posted at the gate. And down there a few bystanders were beginning to loiter, their curiosity roused by the comings and goings: the first trickle of what would become a flood when the lunchtime editions filtered through to the village. What was going through his mind, that stricken-looking man, who an hour earlier had been about to set off to his office? Julia Tallis had gone from the room, probably to get dressed. Of the two, she might prove to be the tougher option ...

Eyke's dabs team arrived and were directed into the garage. Then Bayliss departed with their haul and instructions to the lab. Gently strolled across to the cottage, which was only thirty yards from the house; he could feel Tallis's eye following him. Was it just possible that, in there ...?

He let himself in. A dining-hall gave into a kitchen and a lounge, the latter a bright, comfortable room with big easy chairs and cheerful paintings on the walls. Paul Tallis's belongings lay around: more hi-fi, with an arsenal of cassettes; sailing gear, motoring magazines, binoculars, photographic equipment. A walk-in larder off the kitchen had been converted into a darkroom. Upstairs, one of the bedrooms contained a projector and a screen. Then, in a bedroom with a window facing the harbour, a powerful telescope on a tripod, trained on the sea horizon.

A young man who liked to see and record things ... so what had he seen and recorded just lately?

The projector was loaded; Gently switched it on. But all that flashed on the screen was some shots of yachts. Downstairs, he pondered over the cassettes, among which was a section labelled only with numbers. At a venture he tried the highest number: it was a recording of the last night of the Proms.

Nothing to find ...

But as he replaced the cassette he heard a car draw up outside. Then there was a light step in the porch, and in a moment Paul

Tallis's blue eyes were staring at him.

'What on *earth* is going on here?'

The youngster's gaze was half-indignant, half-alarmed. He stood poised cautiously in the doorway, as though at any instant he might need to take flight.

'Nothing to be afraid of. Come on in!'

'But what are all the people doing here? Cars, policemen … men at the gate. Are you arresting someone or something?'

'Just more routine.'

'But … why are you in here?'

'Part of the job we have to do. Don't worry – it's all in order. What are you doing in Walderness, by the way?'

'Me? I live here, you know!' He relaxed a little, part reassured. 'But I still don't see why you're in the cottage. At least, not without letting me know first.'

Gently shrugged. 'That's how it goes! But don't you have any lectures today?'

'Not till this afternoon. So I thought I'd pop over to see how Fiona was getting on.'

'Ah yes … Miss Quennell.'

'Have you spoken to her?' His eyes held painfully to Gently's.

'No such luck. Have you?'

He shook his head and looked away. 'I called at the house. Auntie Ruth is in a tizzy because the telephone is going all the time – wretched reporters! But Fiona wasn't there, and Auntie Ruth says she's still the same.' He made an odd little gesture. 'Will she ever be better?'

'Perhaps. When the shock has had time to wear off.'

'I don't know … she was never this way before.' He stood a moment staring at the floor. 'Anyway, I came on here, hoping I should get mother on her own. Then I find all this going on, and Uncle Ray's car still in the drive.' He ventured a look. 'What *is* going on?'

'We have to cover every angle, you know.'

'Meaning … Uncle Ray?'

'Even you. Everyone who might have a connection.'

'Even me!'

He laughed shakily, glancing around the pleasant room. It too had an outlook towards the harbour and the picturesque group of riverside buildings. Other windows gave a view of the house, and one could see Raymond Tallis staring hard in their direction. Paul Tallis caught sight of him: the blue eyes tightened.

'He gave you the keys?'

'I requested them.'

'So what does he think you'll find here? That was just a bit of malice on his part, trying to drag me in along with him. He probably thinks I set you on him but you know that isn't true. I've said nothing. And it's nonsense anyway, as I expect you're finding out.'

'What is nonsense?'

'What ...? That Uncle Ray had anything to do with it. To start with he'd scarcely have the nerve, even allowing he had a reason.'

'You think it takes nerve to stab someone?'

Paul Tallis winced. 'W-was it a stabbing?'

'Don't you know?'

'I ... no! Really, only that there'd been foul play. But ... Uncle Freddy was stabbed?'

'Does that suggest something?'

'No, of course not.' He kept shaking his head. 'Only that I was imagining ... I don't know. He could have been battered, perhaps. Or shot.'

'Shot?'

'People do get shot. But you say it was a stabbing ...'

He'd lost a little colour, standing there, his eyes absent, without focus. Today he was dressed in linen slacks and a blazer and a cream shirt wide open at the throat. He looked younger than nineteen: rather like a schoolboy wrestling with some intractable problem. You wanted to throw him a hint, a glimpse of a possible solution ...

Meanwhile, one of the reporters had shifted round from the gate and was leaning over a wall, quizzing the cottage and the Mini. And the onlookers had increased: they included three fishermen who'd come up from the huts on the river wall.

'And ... you're looking for the weapon?'

'Perhaps we've found it.'

'Found it ... about here?'

Gently said nothing.

'I mean ... stabbing ... it could have been anything at all. I expect there are plenty of knives about.'

'Do you have a knife?'

'Actually, yes! I've got a sheath knife about here somewhere ... is that what you're looking for? I think it's in a drawer. I bought it for sailing, but it's scarcely been used.'

The idea seemed almost a relief. He went to forage in drawers in a sideboard, coming up at last with a handsome knife that also embodied a marline-spike and shackle-spanner.

'I wonder you didn't find it ... is it the right sort?'

There was dust between handle and sheath. Gently erected the marline-spike, then snapped it home and handed the knife back.

'The weapon may not have been a knife.'

'Not a knife ...? Then what ...?'

'I'm open to suggestions.'

Just for an instant Paul Tallis teetered; but he shook his head.

'Well, if you could tell me what it was I might know if there's one around the place ...'

Did he know? Perhaps it was only a guess which nothing was going to drag out of him. When the chips were down, the line drawn, Uncle Ray remained family. And there was Julia Tallis of course ... had he done any guessing about her?

Now he had replaced the knife in the drawer and slowly returned into the lounge. He stood for a while staring towards the harbour, ignoring the reporter, who was observing him with interest. He dug hands in the blazer pockets.

'The letter ... that's what you're really here about, isn't it?'

'Do you think so?' Gently asked.

He nodded. 'You still think it was me who took it to The Uplands.'

The hands were poking at the pockets like ramrods and he kept staring through the window in a sort of desperate defiance: a schoolboy with problems that were too much for him. How long was he going to hold out?

'Look — you trapped me into telling you about the letter. You made it seem as though you knew. And I honestly don't know what Fiona had got there, it might have been a pamphlet, something like that.'

'When did you see her with it?'

'Well ... when I got there. I looked for her in the lounge. She was standing by the window with something in her hand, but I couldn't really see what it was.'

'A plain envelope was how you described it.'

'Yes – well, it might have been! But I can't be certain.'

'A plain envelope with no writing on it.'

'None that I saw. I can only say that.'

'But ... an envelope.'

'All right, if it was! You're trying the same game on again. If you're saying it was an envelope, then it was an envelope. But what I'm saying is, I'm not certain.'

He was getting hot-faced and upset, to the absorbed curiosity of the reporter; the latter was edging closer along the wall, which separated the property from the low-lying marsh.

'Didn't you ask her what it was?'

'No. Why should I?'

'It seems a natural enquiry to have made.'

'Well, I didn't. If she'd wanted me to know, no doubt she'd have told me what it was.'

'She had it in her hand, and you went to speak to her?'

'Yes ... no, she put it down somewhere. Now I remember – she put it in a bookcase. That's why I think it may have been a pamphlet.'

'In a bookcase?'

'On top of some books. She just shoved it away as I came over.'

Still the hands were dragging at the pockets and his face was turned obstinately to the window. Across at the house, Raymond Tallis hadn't budged from his post of observation. Eyke had come out of the garage and was sitting in a car, using the RT; as he talked, he too was gazing towards the cottage and at the variegated Mini parked before it.

'What did you talk to her about?'

'I told you. I wanted her to come to the football.'

'That took half an hour?'

'Well ... this and that! I thought perhaps I could have persuaded her to come.'

'But wouldn't you have known she had made other arrangements?'

'Look, I wasn't talking to her about the letter. Of course I knew of her arrangement with mother, they fixed it up during the week.'

'When during the week?'

'What ...? Thursday, probably, when I was taking a load of stuff to the flat. Mother told me Fiona had been here. I expect it was fixed up then.'

'Yet still you tried to persuade her to go to the football?'

'Yes! Look, Fiona often changed her mind. As like as not she would have opted out of that trip. At least, it was worth a try.'

'And you spent half an hour trying to talk her round.'

'Oh, hell, hell!' Paul Tallis beat the pockets against his thighs. 'So you don't believe me, do you? Well, I can't help it. That's how it was, and that's all I can tell you.'

'You could have taken the letter.'

'I could, but I didn't.'

'It probably originated here.'

'That's utter rot!'

'If there were evidence ...?'

'What evidence could there be?'

Shrugging, Gently said nothing.

'You're trying to trap me again,' Paul Tallis said. 'You think I know something and I'll let it out, just as I did at the flat. But I won't, because I don't know anything. Not about the letter or anything else. And if I did I wouldn't cover for anyone ... not after what happened to Uncle Freddy.'

'Nothing about anything,' Gently said.

'Nothing. So stop getting at me.'

After a pause, Gently said: 'Would you remember your grandfather, Walter Tallis?'

'My grandfather ...'

For some moments Paul Tallis had stood silent, the hands in his pockets still, shoulders slightly humped. Then he had turned to face Gently with puzzled but cautious eyes.

'What's he got to do with this?'

'Did you know him?'

'Of course I knew him! Naturally, not very well, because he died when I was about four.'

'Do you remember him dressing up?'

'Dressing up ...?'

'Didn't he have a suit of Lincoln green?'

'A suit ...?'

'Like Robin Hood. Complete with an old-fashioned leather quiver.'

107

Paul Tallis was staring in a frozen sort of way, his neat features set in a half-scowl. He was swaying slightly. He looked round for a chair and dropped into it, rubber-kneed. His voice sounded hoarse.

'What are you getting at now?'

'And your father. Didn't he dress up too?'

'I don't understand ...'

'And your Uncle Raymond. Or perhaps he didn't bother with dressing up?'

Paul Tallis's small mouth hung open; he tried to wet his lips with a dry tongue. His eyes clung to Gently's, huge, like the fearful eyes of a small child.

'You know ... don't you?'

'What do I know?'

'Uncle Raymond ... you think ...'

'What about your uncle?'

Paul Tallis swallowed lumpily. He made a great effort to pull himself together.

'Look, you must tell me how Uncle Freddy died!'

'He died from a wound in his back.'

'Yes, but that's the point, isn't it? You let me believe he was stabbed with a knife.'

'I didn't mention a knife.'

'But you let me believe ...' He swayed in the chair. 'This isn't playing fair, you know. You're trying to get me to say something damning, and after all he is my uncle ... and mother's husband.'

'Do you remember him using a bow?'

Paul Tallis nodded weakly. 'When I was young.'

'And since?'

'No. No!'

'But you've seen him with one?'

'I didn't see anything!' He made an awkward gesture. 'You've got to understand ... all that was over years ago. When I was a kid they all used to shoot, grandad, father, even mother. They set up a target down in the orchard ... the target is still around, somewhere. Father made me hold a bow with him, but of course I wasn't strong enough to pull the string. But mother could manage it. Then grandad died, and they didn't shoot any more after that. It was all a long time ago. And that's as much as I can tell you.'

'What happened to the equipment?'

'There's the target. I think it's up in the garage loft.'

'The bows? The arrows?'

He shook his head. 'Perhaps they were turned out, or given away.'

'If the target was kept, wouldn't they have been?'

He went on shaking his head. 'I know about the target because once I used it for darts. But I don't remember any bows or arrows.'

Gently stared at him. He tried to shape a smile. The hapless eyes wouldn't join in. Yet he couldn't drag his eyes away: he sat like an idiot, his mouth twisting.

'How long since you did a job on your car?'

'My ... car?'

'Wasn't it one day last week?'

'Yes, actually! Points and plugs ... and I checked the timing while I was at it.'

'Which day?'

'Well ... Wednesday evening.'

'In the garage?'

He could only nod.

'You were using a file?'

'No, of course not. Just some fine emery ... the points were pitted.'

'Who else was in there?'

'Nobody – just me!'

'Someone at the vice. Using a file.'

He was trembling. 'No – nothing like that! In fact the others ... they may have been out.'

'Filing brass.'

'Oh lord, no! If Uncle Ray had been there, I'd have cleared out.'

'Instead of which, it was him who cleared out.'

'I tell you no. I didn't *see* Uncle Ray.'

His condition was pitiful. His lips kept trying to smile while his eyes were trapped in a ghastly stare. His wandering hands were ashake, searching, feeling for something not there. It was Gently who broke off the painful séance by going to the window to glare at the reporter. The latter winced, turned away and seemed to find a sudden interest in the harbour.

'What else did you see?'

'Nothing!'

'At precisely what time did you get to Ipswich?'

'I – I … it was around lunchtime.'

'It could have been later. Say after three.'

'But that's not true.'

'It could have been true. Your uncle was up to something suspicious. You thought you'd hang around a little, to see if you could spot what his game was.'

'But I tell you, I didn't!'

'There was this business of the letter. Surely that would have made you curious.'

'Listen, the letter –'

'I know. You didn't take it! And Miss Quennell can't tell us a different story.' Gently rounded from the window. 'When we know so much, what's the point of your lying your head off? Better get it over! You've made your gesture, and now it's time to think about your own skin.'

'My own skin …?'

'If you've guilty knowledge we can pull you in as an accessory.'

'But – but I would never have helped Uncle Ray.'

'One day, Miss Quennell is going to open her mouth.'

Just then it was he who opened his mouth, as though giving vent to a silent cry. Then, childlike, he hid his face with his arm, trying to crouch away from Gently.

'Oh God … I wish my father were alive!'

He seemed more like twelve than nineteen.

'It's unfair … so unfair …!'

You could imagine him in shorts and a round cap with a badge.

And all this while Tallis had never moved from the window of the lounge across the way: humpty-shouldered, face blurred, eyes riveted to the cottage.

'You don't believe anything, do you? It's only what you want to hear! I could tell you all sorts of lies and you'd accept them, if they fitted in … But the truth, what's that to you? Only, of course, you'll get there in the end! But why should it be me …? It simply isn't fair. Why can't you let everything alone?'

'You know I can't do that.'

'When father died, who bothered then? Yet it might have been murder, you don't know.' He gulped. 'They never found *his* body.'

'That was different.'

'He died, didn't he? And only two people to say how. But that was all tea and sympathy, while now even Aunty Ruth ...'

'Mr Quennell's murderer must be punished.'

'Oh, of course – it should never have happened! But it's so unfair ... And everybody's involved. And I don't see why it has to be me ...'

'Are you going to talk to me?'

'No!'

'Perhaps you'd better think about that.'

'I've told you everything, all I'm going to ... I only came here to see mother.'

'You're in a tricky situation.'

'I want to see mother! If you're so certain ... why don't you take him away?'

He jumped up and went to the window to stare back at Raymond Tallis: for the first time the printer's figure wavered, seemed to move back a little into the room.

'It's like a Greek tragedy ...'

'Which one?'

'I don't know! Any one. All those people down at the gate ... they're like the chorus, aren't they?'

By now perhaps thirty gapers had collected and were standing about in watchful groups. The reporters, too, had begun to filter back, probably having twigged that they'd been sent on a wild-goose chase. A couple more were sauntering up along the wall, beside which a footpath ran to the ferry. One was a cameraman: he took a speculative shot of the cottage and the Mini.

'All waiting for something to happen ... but all they'll see is cars leaving.'

'Won't that be tragedy enough for someone?'

'For him, perhaps. And mother.'

'But not for you?'

Paul Tallis was silent, staring at the crowd, which continued to grow. Eyke had sent a man down the drive; he stood looking self-conscious, a few yards inside the gate. A few late visitors, parking for the beach, lingered curious by their cars. The fishermen, standing apart, were smoking and chaffing each other.

'For tragedy, it needs something more ...'

Perhaps you could forgive him, being so young.

'Uncle Ray doesn't seem up to the part ...'

In his young voice was a touch of scorn.

Eyke entered. He was carrying something; he glanced at Gently, then at Paul Tallis. Shrugging, Gently came down the room and went with Eyke into the hall.

'Dabs ...?'

'Afraid not, sir. Just a few blurred smears. But we've photographed the impression, and Hopwood came up with these.'

From an envelope he jigged two small objects on to the cottage dining-table. One was a fragment of curled cinder with scorched feather-web adhering to it. The other, though discoloured by fire, was clearly a tip from one of the arrows. But it was pointed; and rubbing a finger over it, you felt the rough surface left by a file.

'Nothing from the bow ...?'

'It'd be all wood, sir. Reckon he broke it up like he said. But these'll nail him.'

'Better collect the ash and see what the lab can make of it.' He paused, then called: 'Mr Tallis!'

Paul Tallis came out of the lounge. Gently pointed to the two objects. Paul Tallis stared at them, his eyes frightened.

'Do they mean anything to you?'

'No – why should they?'

'They are remnants of an arrow.'

'An arrow ...' His stare was fascinated. 'Oh lord – the incinerator ...'

'What about the incinerator?'

'Nothing!'

'When did you last visit it?'

'I tell you it's nothing. On Saturday evening I was clearing out old papers and took them down there to burn.'

'Who did you see?'

'Nobody. Just that the fire was still smouldering ...'

'Do you have a gardener here on Saturdays?'

Fearfully, Paul Tallis shook his head.

Eyke gazed at the young man with a sort of gruesome benevolence. 'Looks like a full hand, sir ...' he muttered to Gently.

Desperately, Paul Tallis exclaimed: 'But it needn't *mean* anything! Everybody uses the incinerator – it could have been Mrs Potter.'

'She's the domestic,' Eyke said. 'Now you know she leaves early on Saturdays, Mr Paul.'

'But it could have been anyone ... mother ...'

'Just leave it with us, Mr Paul.'

Complacently, Eyke stroked the two objects back into the envelope, on which identification had already been written. Paul Tallis looked on with a helpless expression. His hands crept back into the blazer pockets.

'This is really the end for him, isn't it ...?'

Gently said: 'We shall need a statement from you.'

'Yes, of course ... I understand ...'

'For the moment I want you to stay around – and a word to the wise! Keep away from reporters. You may think I've been tough, but those fellows down there will eat you alive.'

'Yes ... may I talk to mother?'

Gently shrugged. 'Why not?'

'I only thought ...'

Hunching, he drove his hands deeper into the pockets.

They went out of the cottage. At once faces turned in their direction. The reporters were back in force, silently watching, ready to pounce. Raymond Tallis's face was still at the window, beside it now the paler smudge of Julia Tallis. Down at the gate the solitary DC looked a lonely figure as he faced the crowd.

'Better get some uniform men out here.'

'They're on their way, sir. I've just called in.'

'What's at the Quennells'?'

'I've kept a man there.'

'I want that private road sealed off.'

'Yes, sir.' Eyke nodded to the window. 'Are we going to have them in?'

'Not quite yet.'

Eyke's grey eyes questioned.

'Fiona Quennell makes the nap hand.'

10

The sky, which earlier had been so brilliant, now was clouding over from the south-west, and a puffy breeze was ruffling the poplars that lined the private road leading to The Uplands. By luck they had intercepted the minibus bringing in the contingent of uniform men, and Eyke had posted two constables with a row of cones to bar the road to the trailing reporters.

At the gate of The Uplands a DC waved them down.

'Sir, Mr Reymerston is at the house. I didn't know whether I should let him by, but Mrs Quennell made a special point of it.'

'How long has he been here?'

'Half an hour, sir.'

'Has Miss Quennell come by?'

'She went out on her bike at half nine, sir, but I haven't seen her come back.'

'What about Frank Quennell?'

'As far as I know he's at home, sir.'

They drove on in. Beside Ruth Quennell's Mini stood Reymerston's blue Renault; and there was also a woman's bicycle, leaning against the garage wall.

'Reckon she's about here, sir,' Eyke said. 'Perhaps we should send a man round the back.'

After a moment, Gently shook his head. 'Either she's ready to talk, or she isn't.'

At the door they were met by Frank Quennell. The young man stood blocking their entry.

'Look – you've got to give us better protection! The press were swarming here yesterday afternoon ...'

'You won't be troubled by them again.'

'But it's getting so that mother daren't go out. And the phone never stops ringing ... we've had to leave it off the hook ...'

'Is your sister in, Mr Quennell?'

'What's that got to do with it?' A gleam came into his eye. 'So it

114

wasn't such foolishness after all, was it, having a go at Uncle Raymond! I'm not just a pretty face, you know. I had this business weighed up from the start. Since Saturday he's been slinking about like a thief, not daring to look me in the eye ...'

'Mr Quennell –'

'It was pretty obvious, wasn't it? You just had to ask who stood to gain most. And all you could think about was mother, because she happened to have a friend. Well, who's looking foolish now? Perhaps another time you'll give a little credit ...'

Gently stared at the burly young man, whose full cheeks were certainly destined to give rise to jowls.

'Talking of people who stand to gain! Aren't you one of those yourself, Mr Quennell?'

'I – what?'

'You were your father's assistant, and I don't hear of any other active directors. If Mr Tallis should be removed your prospects would appear to be better than good.'

Frank Quennell's eyes popped. 'But that's ridiculous!'

'It is in your interest to have suspicion fall on Mr Tallis.'

'Listen, just because it so happens –'

'I wish to speak to your mother, Mr Quennell.'

Looking shaken, Frank Quennell fell back and permitted Gently and Eyke to enter the hall. Gently knocked at the door of the lounge; it was opened by Reymerston. Ruth Quennell was the only other occupant.

Today the flowers in the grate were Michaelmas daisies and the odour of the room that of Reymerston's Scotch mixture. Pipe in mouth, he greeted Gently with one of his slow, sardonic smiles. Ruth Quennell sat by the hearth; she was wearing a dark costume, a semi-mourning. She gazed up at Gently as he entered, her eyes full of question.

'Is it true then ... about Ray?'

'He is helping our enquiries, Mrs Quennell.'

'But isn't that the same thing as saying ...?' She let it trail, still holding his eye.

Reymerston said: 'I came by the Lodge and couldn't help noticing the excitement. I thought it was time to brief Ruth on the direction things might take.'

'We have made some progress at the Lodge.'

'Oh heavens,' Ruth Quennell groaned. 'Poor Julie. But I can't believe it. Ray just isn't that sort of man.'

'You know him very well, Mrs Quennell.'

'I've known Ray for twenty-five years. He isn't a saint, but on the other hand there's nothing really bad about him. It's his manner really ... and a certain weakness.' She looked down at the flowers. 'He's made passes at me, too, though not so often since he married Julie. He always wanted Julie. Perhaps because Arthur saw her first.'

'He has lived in his brother's shadow.'

'Yes. Ray is fundamentally a younger brother.'

'A jealous younger brother.'

She gestured. 'Simply, one can't believe it of him.'

She looked more drawn and colourless today; it might have been that the costume didn't suit her complexion. Reymerston, who had come across to sit by her, was watching her face with a trace of concern.

Gently said: 'It is important for me to see Fiona, Mrs Quennell. Somehow that letter got to your husband, and it may be that your daughter can tell us how.'

'Fiona can't tell you.'

'Still, I must see her.'

Ruth Quennell shook her head, her expression determined. 'I guessed what it was you'd come for. I told Andy. But nobody is going to see Fiona.'

'Is she in the house?'

'We have consulted Dr Grey and he says positively that she's not to be troubled.'

'I can promise you –'

'Oh, I know. But it makes no difference.' Her mouth was trembling. 'Fiona wouldn't have done it, not even if she'd thought it was a silly prank. She didn't love her father but she never went against him. She always treated him with respect.'

'Even so, the letter –'

'She couldn't have done it. I've been thinking of nothing else. She wasn't near her father all morning, and at lunch she was first to leave the table.'

'But if she passed by him?'

'She didn't pass by him. He was sitting at the top end of the table. She went straight out and up the stairs, and I heard her moving about in her room. Fiona didn't do it because she couldn't – and nobody is going to upset her.'

She bit tightly on her lips and made an odd little keening sound. Reymerston reached out to touch her arm but she put his hand away. Nevertheless she seemed close to tears. She kept her face turned towards the flowers.

'The letter originated at Caxton Lodge.'

He could hear her gasp. 'I can't believe that!'

'We have evidence in proof.'

'But who?' Now she faced him, her eyes large.

'Perhaps the style suggests the author.'

'The style ...? Oh heavens ... not Julie!' Her eyes were shocked. 'This is too much. How can I believe that such things have gone on?'

'Last week, how many times was your daughter at Caxton Lodge?'

Ruth Quennell groaned. 'Oh no.'

'Was she there on Thursday?'

Ruth Quennell nodded.

'That day she was alone with Mrs Tallis.'

'Alone with her ... are you suggesting ...?'

Gently stared at her in silence.

'There's logic in it,' Reymerston said quietly. 'It isn't so, but there's logic in it.'

Ruth Quennell stared wildly, her lips quivering, her face long. 'Paul! It has to be Paul.'

'I have questioned Paul, Mrs Quennell.'

'He was here on Saturday morning – it's the only possible way.'

'I believe he went nowhere near your husband.'

'But he could have left the letter for Freddy to find.'

'To convince Mr Quennell he must seem to have dropped it. To do that he must have been in Mr Quennell's vicinity.'

'But you don't know he wasn't.'

'By your own account Paul Tallis was here and your husband down the garden. That agrees with his own account. Your daughter's account we still await.'

'But – I could have been wrong.'

'You were in the kitchen?'

'Yes, but all the same –'

'With the door open?'

She nodded helplessly.

'To get to the back Paul Tallis would have to pass by either the kitchen door or the kitchen window, and return by one or other of the same routes. Could you have remained unaware of that?'

'Yes – it's possible.'

'But how probable?'

'I don't care – I know it was Paul.'

'According to him he saw your daughter with an envelope in her hand.'

'Then he was lying – he was lying!'

'Is Paul Tallis a liar?'

'Why wouldn't he lie if he was in this dreadful plot against Freddy?'

'But ... would he have been in such a plot?'

'Oh God – and would my daughter?'

Reymerston murmured: 'There's a point there, you know. Old Paul was something of a buddy of Freddy's.'

'I know. I know. And I can't help it. Anything is possible except that Fiona ...'

'You've always reckoned Paul a decent kid.'

'He is, I don't deny it. Oh Andy, I'm so confused. It's as though the ground were opening under my feet.'

Reymerston turned to Gently. 'Isn't it just possible that somebody has put it across these kids? If it were Julia Tallis who concocted that letter, it's worth remembering the influence she'd have with them. Paul would lie himself stupid for his mother, and Fiona would feel obliged to stand by them. Only in her case the shock of discovery has been too great: she'd been made an instrument in the killing of a father.'

Gently said: 'Can you suggest a way they could have been imposed on?'

'Not off the cuff. But it must have been possible.'

'Possible – but credible?'

Reymerston shrugged faintly. 'When it's a woman like Julia Tallis.'

Ruth Quennell burst out: 'I just can't believe any of it, not however hard I try! Julia isn't a sort of Lady Macbeth, and Ray – well, I've always felt *sorry* for him. And Paul – oh dear, Paul! He's just a silly, passionate boy. He's fond of Fiona, and she's fond of him ... there's just no reason for any of this.'

118

'Yet somewhere there's a reason,' Reymerston said. 'Somewhere there has to be a reason.'

'Well, it isn't to do with us – not any of us.' She began to cry with a sort of half-controlled hysteria. 'We aren't murderers – we're just ordinary people, people trying to live a decent life – weak people, perhaps, but only weak: not wicked! And something's happened – I don't know what's happened – I don't know how it *could* have happened ... just like poor Arthur getting drowned. Only this time ... this time ...'

'Hush,' Reymerston said. 'Hush, Ruth. It'll all come right. It must come right. But we'll have to help him. He's a compassionate man, I know him. We've got to help.'

'Andy – I'm so afraid. Everything seems to be going to pieces.'

'It'll come right, Ruth. We'll make it come right. I know, because I've been through it all before.'

She cried for a time; he held her hand tightly. In the rest of the house there was silence. Somewhere out there was Frank Quennell, probably the domestic, and ... in her room ...? But all was silence. Outside, you could hear the breeze lilting in the copper beech.

At last she contained her sobbing.

'Then ... there's nothing for it. You must see her?'

'If I may, Mrs Quennell.'

'But what's the use ... in the way she is?'

'I must still try.'

'It could make her worse.'

'You may stop me whenever you please.'

'Couldn't you let me question her?'

Gently hesitated. Then he nodded. 'In my presence.'

Ruth Quennell snuffled and produced a handkerchief from her sleeve. After dabbing her eyes and face she rose, stared a moment at Gently, then left the room. They heard her feet on the stairs and the opening of a door above.

Reymerston said: 'You know, what scares her is that Fiona might really have had a hand in it. Fiona has never properly got over the shock of Arthur Tallis's death.' He glanced at Gently. 'That's not the idea, is it?'

Gently hunched. 'That's one alternative.'

'Oh, for God's sake!' Reymerston said. 'It was her own father, remember.'

'Apparently Arthur Tallis also meant a great deal to her.'

'But no blame ever attached to Quennell. You can think what you like about Raymond Tallis, but Quennell came out with a clean sheet.'

'According to Raymond Tallis it was Quennell who tailored their evidence.'

'But that's what you'd expect him to say,' Reymerston retorted warmly. 'Quennell isn't here to give him the lie. But mark this – young Paul didn't blame Quennell: they were on the same footing as before. It's easy to guess who Paul blames, and that would go for Fiona too.'

'As I said ... one alternative.'

'Not an alternative to waste much time over.'

Gently said: 'Mrs Tallis and Fiona Quennell would have passed the gorse circle approximately at the time of Quennell's death.'

Reymerston sat very straight. 'You're not serious about that.'

'It's a fact on the table.' Gently shrugged. 'Here's another. We've identified the weapon. It was one that Mrs Tallis had practice in using.'

'The weapon!'

'It wasn't a knife.'

For a while Reymerston stared, eyes intent. Then he shook his head. 'This is beyond me. But all my instinct says you're wrong. Me, I'm not siding with Julia Tallis, who for all I know is Messalina's cousin. But when you try to link her with Fiona Quennell, then my instinct kicks. Fiona doesn't fit. She may be disturbed, but at the bottom she's a gentle, affectionate kid. She would no more plot and plan murder than a bishop would cheat at cards. Nor do I believe you truly think so.'

Gently said: 'I've seen her three times. Once at the gorse circle, twice staring at the windows of Caxton Lodge. And each time she ran.'

'Fiona is innocent.'

'But what there is to know, she knows.'

'She's still innocent.'

Gently said nothing. Reymerston went on staring at him.

They heard steps on the stairs, a hesitation and low voices. Then Ruth Quennell entered along with her daughter and Frank Quennell.

'Where's daddy?'

Fiona Quennell spoke it in a tone so completely natural that for a moment you were almost glancing about the room, seeking to locate the absent man. Her manner too seemed entirely tranquil. She followed her mother into the room. Smilingly, Reymerston rose to give her his chair, and Fiona Quennell graciously accepted it.

'Where's daddy?'

'Hush, Oona!'

Ruth Quennell sat by her daughter's side. Her face was still smeary from crying; her eyes were fixed anxiously on her daughter.

'Those two men are policemen, aren't they?'

'They are here to help us, darling.'

'Oh, yes. Because we've lost daddy.'

'Hush, darling. They are kind men.'

Fiona Quennell stared at Gently. Her intense brown eyes had no expression. Seen closer, her smooth, full-cheeked face suggested a ripe fruit, firm, flawless. Her straight dark hair was brushed back and caught up loosely behind with a ribbon. She was strongly built. She was wearing a short skirt that revealed well-muscled legs.

'Have they found daddy?'

'They are helping us, darling, and we must try to help them too.'

'I don't think daddy's going to come back. I think he's gone away with a friend.'

Frank Quennell had remained by the door, where he stood gazing frowningly at his sister. Reymerston had taken a seat on the settee. Eyke, as ever, held the background.

'Listen, darling. We're trying to remember. Every little thing that happened on Saturday. What daddy did, what we did. Even the tiniest thing might help.'

'Oh, I don't think it would. He's gone with a friend, and he wouldn't tell anyone about that.'

'But we must try, darling.'

Fiona Quennell sat silently scrutinising Gently.

'Mummy, who is that man?'

'Oona, darling –'

'He isn't one of ours. I keep seeing him about everywhere, and always he's staring at me.'

'He's from London, darling. He's a nice man.'

'I don't think he's nice at all.'

'He's kind and he's helping us.'

Fiona Quennell sat silently staring. At last she said brightly:

'I bought a dress, you know. Aunty Julie took me in. And there was this peculiar woman in the shop, I think she was one of those. Do you think she could have been? Aunty Julie thought so. She was all over me in the fitting-room. There was a teacher sacked for it at Huntingfield, but that was when I was in the fourth.' She paused. 'But daddy wasn't with us. So why does that man keep looking at me?'

'Oona, please –'

'I'm sure he shouldn't be here. Daddy wouldn't want him in the house.'

'Hush, darling, hush!'

'He's up to no good. Mummy, I think you should ask him to leave.'

Ruth Quennell looked helplessly at Gently, who shrugged and felt in his pocket for his pipe. He stuck it empty in his mouth. Fiona Quennell watched every move.

'Darling, try to remember a little more. What were we doing on Saturday morning?'

'I think daddy has gone to London and he's living there with a friend. That's all right, isn't it? I mean there isn't a law against it. Aunty Julie thinks it's all right. But I'm never going to get married, mummy.'

'Darling, on Saturday –'

'I shall live alone. I'm going a long way away. I don't want to see anyone. I don't want to get married.'

'Oh, darling.'

'They can't make me, you know. I needn't get married unless I want to. And I don't want to! I want to be alone. But I'll write you letters when I get there.'

'Oh, darling, where?'

'Where I'm going. Somewhere very far away. But you needn't worry, I shall be all right, you don't have to worry about me any more.'

'Oona, oh Oona!'

'It's all right, mummy. Don't cry in front of that wicked man.'

Frank Quennell said: 'You've got to stop this. Can't you see what you're doing to her?'

Blank-faced, Gently chewed on his pipe, staring back into Fiona Quennell's unwinking eyes. They hadn't once faltered. Words were coming from her mouth as though they had no reference to those wide-open eyes.

'Frank, don't interfere!'

'My sister's being crucified. The police have got no right –'

Dabbing at her eyes, Ruth Quennell jogged herself straighter in her chair.

'Oona, listen to me. You've got to remember. Paul called when daddy was down the garden.'

'I don't like that dress, mummy. Aunty Julie liked it , but I don't think it suits me. Aunty Julie –'

'Listen to me, Oona!'

'I don't think daddy would have liked it –'

'Oona, I'm asking you. When Paul called, what were you talking about in here?'

And for the first time the eyes flickered ...

'Of course it can come out of my allowance, but I'm never going to wear it. Daddy was in the garden, he always is, daddy talks to Jackson on Saturdays ...'

'Did Paul give you something?'

'I told Aunty Julie, the dress wasn't really my colour at all, I prefer greens and tans, blues don't go with my complexion. She said why not try something different, but I'm never, never going to wear it, daddy would have agreed, daddy liked me best in green.' Her eyes slid. 'I saw him from my window.'

'Who did you see from your window?'

'When I was doing my essay he went down the garden to talk to Jackson. They got the ladder from the shed and Jackson went up into the tree, but that was before I bought the dress, daddy never actually saw it.'

'Oona, answer me! What did Paul give you?'

'I'm never going to get married, mummy.'

'What did he tell you to do with it?'

'I'm going a long way away.'

'Stop it, stop it!' Frank Quennell cried. 'Leave Oona alone, just let her be.'

'Daddy's in London,' Fiona Quennell said. 'They say he's dead, but he isn't really. He's gone to London with his friend. I expect he's gone for a long time. We may not even see him again, perhaps he won't write me a letter. But he isn't dead, they only say that. On Saturday he was picking apples in the garden.' She smiled suddenly. 'It's a mistake, you know. It wasn't daddy who was killed at all.'

'Oh God, God,' Frank Quennell cried. 'Mother, will you let it go on? This is Oona, this is my sister. For pity's sake don't push her any further.'

Ruth Quennell threw an anguished look at Gently: Gently went on chewing his pipe.

'I shall give the dress to Oxfam,' Fiona Quennell said. 'That'll be best. It was quite an expensive dress, but that's what daddy would have done. I shall write them a letter, a letter, a letter. Perhaps daddy will write me a letter. Then I shall write him a letter. Then he will write me a letter. A letter, a letter. I've never had many letters.'

'Oona,' Frank Quennell groaned. 'My little sister.'

'When I go away, I shall write letters. Only I may not be able to post them, I'll need a friend to smuggle them out. That's how it's done, isn't it? People smuggle them out for you. But who's going to smuggle them out for daddy?' Her mouth puckered. 'I shall write to mummy, Frank and Aunty Julie.'

Round his pipe Gently said: 'But not to Paul Tallis?'

One could hear the sharp hiss of her breath. She slanted herself a little away from him, leering from the corners of her eyes.

'Listen – there's daddy's car!'

But it was only the soughing of the beech.

'When daddy comes he'll turn that man out. He won't let him sit there watching me. I knew him from the first, he's a wicked person. He's come here to do evil things. But I know him, it's no good him watching me. Mummy, why don't you send him away?'

Gently said: 'I can't be sent away.'

The posture of her body was becoming a crouch. She made a hissing noise at Gently; her leer was full of a naïve malevolence.

'Oh, stop it, stop it!' Frank Quennell cried.

Fiona Quennell had a little foam at her mouth. Very slowly, Gently reached into his pocket and took out the envelope from Julia Tallis's bureau. He held it towards Fiona Quennell.

'This is the letter Paul Tallis gave you.'

She was groaning and spitting at him, her flinching eyes darting hatred.

'So what did you do with it?'

She mowed and chattered and threatened him with hooked fingers. Then, in a flash, she sprang from the chair, seized the envelope and rushed to the door.

'Follow her – see what she does with it.'

Frank Quennell pelted after his sister. Their steps hammered down the hall and entered the kitchen; there was a scuffle, a clapping sound, the slam of a door. Frank Quennell returned; he had the envelope.

'Well?'

'She dumped it – in the swing-bin.'

'The swing-bin!' Ruth Quennell's hand flew to her mouth. 'Freddy went to the swing-bin – he went to it after lunch on Saturday.' She rounded on Gently. 'You remember – I told you! He went to the bin to scrape out his pipe. And he stayed there in the kitchen ... oh lord, he must have seen the letter ...'

'So she didn't pass it on,' Frank Quennell burst out. 'They tried to use Oona, but she wouldn't have it.'

'Oh, she's innocent,' Ruth Quennell cried. 'Oona is innocent, I knew she was innocent.'

'Mother – it must have been Paul.'

'Oh my daughter, my daughter,' Ruth Quennell sobbed.

'Yes, Paul,' Frank Quennell said. 'But why? Why?'

Reymerston said to Gently: 'He'll never peach on his mother.'

Gently went on chewing his pipe.

11

'So now we know, sir,' Eyke said.

Gently grunted and adjusted his seat-strap. Outside, yesterday's bright day had definitely vanished and a smeary wrack was passing over the sun. Every so often a stronger puff was rattling leaves and setting sprays swinging, yet the atmosphere was hot and sticky. One felt that a brisk shower would be a relief.

Gently said: 'See what Ipswich have got.'

Eyke activated the RT.

'Nothing yet, sir.' He glanced sideways at Gently. 'Do you reckon young Paul is in it up to his neck?'

Gently sat sullenly watching the tossing leaves, his empty pipe still in his mouth. Finally he shoved the pipe away, felt for his key and started the engine.

At the junction they had to pause while the cones were shifted to let them through; at once reporters clustered to the window and the eyes of cameras winked.

'No comment yet.'

'Listen, Chiefie, we've been having a word with young Tallis –'

'Lay off young Tallis –'

'He says the weapon was a bow and arrow, and that his uncle –'

'If you print that I'll have you.'

'Chiefie, Tallis is an ex-member –'

Gently slammed up his window and drove on, leaving the reporters diving for their cars.

'The bloody young fool.'

There was no doubt now where the centre of interest lay in Walderness. Cars were parked all along the green and people were hastening down towards the house. There a TV van had parked and a camera was panning round the scene: a thrusting young man with a microphone almost committed suicide in front of the car.

'Chief Superintendent Gently, sir, a comment on the progress of the case!'

Behind him the camera settled and a man wearing earphones twiddled the controls.

'Very well, then. This morning we have made certain progress with the assistance of local people. We now have a clearer picture of important aspects of the case.'

'There is talk of you finding the weapon, sir.'

'I can make no comment at this stage.'

'Sir, would it be correct to say that you anticipate an arrest?'

'A fuller statement will be issued later.'

He conjured up a half-smile, then jammed the car through the gate. There were no faces at any windows now, and a uniform man stood guarding the steps. Gently rattled to a halt. Across at the cottage, the figure of Paul Tallis hastily withdrew from the porch.

'Let's talk to him.'

They strode over. Paul Tallis waited fearfully in the hall. He shrank from them as they entered, his blue eyes big with fright.

'I couldn't help it ...!'

'I thought I told you not to talk to the reporters.'

'Two of them got over the wall. I didn't want to talk to them. They seemed to know it all, anyway.'

'And you fell for that?'

'I thought you must have told them – they kept saying it was a matter of record. Honestly I didn't tell them much, just that you'd taken away bits of an arrow.'

'And that your uncle was an archer!'

'They seemed to know about that ...'

'What else did you tell them?'

'Nothing, I swear. Some policemen arrived and they went off ...'

Gently stared at the shrinking figure. Paul Tallis attempted a ghastly smile. But he was trembling. He hadn't even dared to stick his hands in the blazer pockets.

'You've been to see Fiona ...'

'Sit down.'

Paul Tallis half-collapsed on a dining-room chair. Gently took a seat on the refectory table, looking down at the young man.

'Now. Have you seen your mother?'

'Mother has nothing to do with this!'

'But have you seen her?'

He gazed about helplessly. 'Look ... you've got it all wrong about mother. She's in a terrible state, crying, wailing ... you might think she's tough, but she isn't really. She's trying to think of all the people who've been here and who might have made use of her bureau – accusing them right, left and centre. It's dreadful, what you've done to mother.'

'What sort of people?'

'I don't know! Friends of hers who pop in and out. Mother has lots of friends. She's been on the phone, ringing some of them. And it isn't fair, you know. You're trying to make her crack and come out with something. But she wouldn't, even if she knew it, and you've got to stop badgering her.'

'The letter was written at her bureau.'

'All right – if you say so. She's ready to admit it. But not by her. She wouldn't do it to Aunty Ruth – what sort of person do you think she is?'

'Then if she didn't write it, who did?'

'She isn't the only person who lives here.'

'Are we talking about your uncle?'

Paul Tallis evaded his eye. 'She'll never give him away, don't you think it.'

'And of course ... you won't.'

'No, I won't! After all, he is mother's husband. I know we don't get on and all that, but you have to draw a line somewhere.'

'Even to put your mother in the clear.'

Paul Tallis rolled his shoulders in frustration. 'You've got to believe me. She didn't do it. She doesn't know anything about this at all.'

'You know that for a fact?'

In a small voice he said: 'All right, then ... I know it for a fact.'

'That's progress, at least.'

Gently paused, surveying Paul Tallis's scowling face. The young man wasn't trembling now, but the blue eyes were staring hopelessly at nothing. Again you were looking at the schoolboy who had bitten off more than he could chew.

'Fiona ... did you see her?'

'Yes, I saw Miss Quennell.'

'She's ... all right?'

'She's in good hands.'

'Did she ... was there any message for me?'

'No message.'

He made a fluttery gesture. 'You know what I mean!'

'I think I know what you mean.'

'It's terrible, her being like this. Really, Fiona is the only person ...'

' ... who understands you?'

'Yes, if you like! Till now it has always been her and me. I could depend on her. And now ... suddenly ... it's as though I were quite alone.'

'You're forgetting your mother.'

'Never mind mother! Perhaps she has never understood me anyway. Not that I blame her, don't think that, but she's never let me come close to her. Mother likes people of her own age ... men. Fiona's the only one I've been close to.'

'No doubt your father seemed very remote.'

'He was a man, that's different. When I was young he used to play with me and take an interest in what I did. Later on he was wrapped up in the business but he mostly took me on the yacht. He was a *real* man. I wanted to grow up like him. But that's not the same, of course.'

'Fiona too ...'

'She loved father. I tell you, father was a different breed.' He bit his lip. 'When Uncle Ray took over it was rather like bad money driving out good.'

'That's hard on your uncle.'

'I know, I know. And perhaps I understand it ... now.'

He stared away through the open door to where the uniform man stood guarding the house; then he gave a little shudder. From the direction of the gate one could hear the murmuring of the crowd.

'I despise him for taking father's place. But I don't want him to go to prison.'

Gently said: 'I am now convinced that you took the letter to Fiona Quennell.'

'Does she ... say that?'

Gently was silent. Paul Tallis's beseeching eyes were fixed on his.

'If I did, would I be an accessary?'

'Only if you knew what the letter was about.'

'As though I would have done it, knowing that! I would have

stuffed the letter down his throat first.' He hesitated. 'What did she do with it?'

'Fiona Quennell tried to get rid of it. But Mr Quennell found it and apparently convinced himself it was genuine.'

'Oh lord – poor Uncle Freddy. He must have been fated to get it somehow.' His mouth quivered. 'It's ironic, really. And then he walked straight into the trap ...'

'Why did you take it?'

'I haven't admitted –' He broke off. 'But it's no good, is it? If Fiona told you, you're bound to believe her. And I'm not going to call Fiona a liar.'

'So?'

'Well ... I took it, then. Uncle Ray said it was a joke on Uncle Freddy. It was supposed to be a letter from his girl-friend to Aunty Ruth, saying it was time they had a talk. He wanted me to leave it where Uncle Freddy would find it, but Uncle Freddy was down the garden, so I left it with Fiona. Neither of us thought it was very funny.'

To the ceiling Gently said: 'You're lying.'

'But that's *exactly* what happened!'

Gently shook his head. 'Suddenly, you're willing to assist your uncle in a dubious joke?'

'Yes – he was always playing practical jokes! I mean, you just have to ask anyone –'

'With you giving him a hand?'

'Well – yes. That is ... sometimes.'

'Only this wasn't a joke.'

'I didn't know that.'

'And it wasn't your uncle who gave you the letter.'

Paul Tallis trembled on the chair. He opened his mouth, but didn't speak. Like a child caught out in a fib, he could only stare with appalled eyes.

'Then it was your mother.'

'No. No!'

'The alternative is that you wrote it yourself.'

'Oh lord, lord.'

'Which way do you want it?'

'You've got it wrong – all wrong.'

'Not your mother and not you.'

'You just lead me on into a trap. It isn't fair, I'm not a lawyer, you can twist me round your little finger.'

'But after all that, it was your mother?'

'I didn't say so and I'm not saying anything! I'm taking it all back, everything I've said, and I'm not making any wretched statement.'

Gently shrugged. 'You'll have to make one in court.'

'Why should I? This is nothing to do with me.'

'That's the statement you'll have to make in court if I decide to put you up as accessary.'

'I won't tell lies about mother ...'

'Just once you could try the truth.'

The blue eyes sparked fire, but Paul Tallis's mouth set tight and small. Emotionally, without doubt, he was a good deal younger than his age. Because of a mother like Julia Tallis ...? The neat features might almost have been those of a girl. An admired father, many leagues above him, and, for comrade, an unstable girl ...

'I've done what you wanted, haven't I?'

His voice was choked with bitterness.

'What have you done?'

'Given mother away. Now you can go and hammer at her, too.'

'So your mother did give you the letter.'

His hands dithered in front of him. 'Oh – what's the use! Look, suppose it was me who wrote the letter ... couldn't you go along with that?'

'Why would you write it?'

'I don't know – to kid Fiona, anything you like. Not to upset Uncle Freddy, Uncle Freddy got hold of it by accident. Look, it's quite plausible ...'

Gently stared long at him, then shook his head.

'But it's quite possible.'

'Not unless it was you at the gorse circle.'

Paul Tallis's mouth crumpled like a small boy's. 'Then you're going ahead ... with mother too.'

Gently said nothing. Paul Tallis crouched, holding himself in.

'What will happen to them?'

Then he was sobbing.

'You can't do it – you can't do it!'

Eyke stirred uncomfortably and looked away: at the gate now there was a regular jamboree. An ice-cream van had pulled up with tinkling chimes, and the reporters were rushing to be first in the queue.

Gently said:

'I want you to stay here. And you will make no more statements to reporters.'

'But I've got lectures –'

'Give me your car keys.'

Sniffling, Paul Tallis handed them over.

'Mayn't I see mother ...'

'Later.'

'Now – please, just once!'

'You will stay here.'

His tear-glazed eyes implored Gently, but he said no more. They went from the cottage.

A scared-eyed woman wearing a pinafore opened the door of the house to them. In the lounge, Raymond Tallis and his wife sat together on the settee, holding hands. Curtains had been drawn at the principal windows, leaving only one to provide light. The couple didn't stir when Gently and Eyke entered but remained gazing into each other's eyes.

Gently said:

'It is in order for you to have a lawyer present.'

They took no notice. In the dim light, it was difficult to see their expressions.

'I may as well warn you that anything you say may be taken down and used in evidence.'

Still their hands stayed clasped, their eyes fixed each on each. Finally Raymond Tallis said thickly:

'What does it matter? I'm done for, anyway.'

'Is that a confession?'

'Look out there. I can't live on here after this.'

'Oh, it's wicked!' Julia Tallis whimpered. 'We're being crucified, that's what. And why? On some pretended evidence. As though we would do such a thing to Freddy.'

'The evidence is being evaluated. What I require from you now are statements.'

'Only so you can tie us in tighter. You've made up your mind that we did it.'

'I believe you forged that letter, Mrs Tallis.'

'I didn't – I didn't! It might have been anyone.'

'I believe you gave it to your son with certain instructions, and that he passed it on to Fiona Quennell.'

Her eyes were horrified in the shadow. 'Is that what he says? Paul says that?'

'I have questioned your son and Miss Quennell.'

'But ... if he says that, then he's protecting Fiona.'

'I think that unlikely.'

'But yes – can't you see? It has to be her who wrote the letter. I don't know why – she isn't normal! – but that's the only explanation. And Paul would know, and he's protecting her.' She sobbed. 'If he had to choose between us, he'd choose her.'

'He'd choose me for the chop,' Raymond Tallis said. 'Not you, Julie. Me. That's who he's aiming at. He'd try to keep you out of it. Don't believe all this man is telling you.'

'But if Paul said that –'

'He'll take it back.'

'Oh Ray, I'm so frightened.'

'Just keep your head.'

She moaned. Raymond Tallis put his arm round her, hugging her. He looked at Gently.

'Are you taking me in?'

'I require the presence of both of you at the police station.'

'Oh no,' Raymond Tallis said. 'Not her. You're not taking her through that mob.'

'I regret I must insist.'

'You're not having her. Julie's been through too much already. And she's nothing to do with it, do you hear me? Julie is outside what happened here.'

He was sitting up straight, suddenly belligerent, as though he'd taken on Gently single-handed. Julia Tallis moaned and clung to him, her face buried in his shoulder.

'What is it that she's outside of?'

'That letter, for a start. I can guess what Paul said about it, and it wasn't that he had it from her.'

'Are you saying you gave it to him?'

'I'm saying nothing! But that'd be closer to the mark. I know Paul and his little games, and my neck is the one that's sticking out. And I don't care, do you understand? I'm past it now, past caring. You can put a noose round my neck and welcome, only don't think I'm going to help you do it.'

'Oh Ray, no,' Julia Tallis wailed. 'If Paul says that it's both of us.'

'Paul didn't say that.'

'Ray, you mustn't!'

'Keep your head, girl,' Raymond Tallis muttered.

Julia Tallis brushed away tears. 'Perhaps I haven't been the best of mothers for Paul,' she groaned. 'It was losing my daughter, I don't know, for a time I couldn't seem to give him attention.'

'You mustn't blame yourself, Julie.'

'Somehow I just wanted to make up for it, not to be a mother or even a wife, only to have a good time.' She sniffed. 'I neglected Paul. That's why he clung to me so hard. He doesn't love me, not really. It may even be better if I'm taken away.'

'Julie, Julie.'

'I'm not a good woman. I probably deserve all that's coming. I wasn't faithful to Arthur. Arthur knew it. He despised me, but he didn't punish me.'

'Julie, shut up!'

'And now my own son points a finger at his mother. I should never have married you, Ray. We could just have gone on, but I shouldn't have married you.'

Raymond Tallis sent a desperate glance at Gently. One felt he was near to shaking his wife. She grumbled and moaned on his shoulder, fingers digging into his arm. He pushed her away. She covered her face and sobbed and wailed without let.

'Look – I'll do a deal with you. Take me in, but leave her.'

'I need statements from you both.'

'Do it my way, and I'll make it easy for you.'

'No!' Julia Tallis gasped.

Raymond Tallis's face was flushing with anger. 'You'll just keep quiet, Julie, and let me handle this how I see fit.'

'But it's no use, Ray, no use.'

'Do as I say, woman. Hold your tongue.'

'I won't let you, Ray.'

He paused, then fetched her a ringing smack across the cheek. 'Ohhh!'

She sat still with shock; and Raymond Tallis was looking shocked too. After a moment he felt for her hand, and, hesitantly, she gave it to him. And again in the gloom they were gazing at each other: Julia Tallis swallowing a sob.

'There's a case against me – I know that. And there may be things you haven't told me yet. Look at it one way, and I had a motive for getting rid of old Freddy. He knew the answers to a lot of questions that people ask themselves about me – slanderous questions I don't deserve, and nobody now to give them the lie. So it's my word and that's not good enough. And all the circumstances are against me. I could have set it up, I had opportunity, for all I know the weapon was around here: I'm right in the middle. And my character won't save me – I married the wife of the brother I may have drowned.'

'Oh no, Ray, no,' Julia Tallis cried.

Raymond Tallis stroked her hand, then squeezed it tight.

'So that's how you see it, how you're right to see it, because Freddy's killer must be put away. So what I'm saying is, let's get on with it – charge me, and put it to the test. I'm ready for it. I'm going to fight. I don't want it swept under the carpet. But leave Julia out. She's an innocent woman, take my word for that if for nothing else.' He stared fiercely at Gently. 'What do you say?'

Blank-faced, Gently said: 'I can't do that.'

'But why?'

'Either Mrs Tallis wrote that letter or she was instrumental in securing its delivery.'

'But I'm telling you she wasn't!'

'Then tell me the alternative.'

'The alternative ...' Raymond Tallis rocked his bowed shoulders. 'Fiona. Fiona could have done it. Look at the way she keeps hanging round me.'

'Not Fiona.'

'So you tell me.'

'I think we both know an obvious author, Mr Tallis.'

'Me, you're saying!'

Gently shrugged: Julia Tallis set up a wail.

'All right, then – me, if you want it that way. I'm willing to shoulder it with the rest! So say I wrote it and gave it to Paul – he'll certainly be ready to back me up.'

'You wish to implicate Paul?'

Raymond Tallis squirmed. 'He wouldn't know what it was about – a bit of a lark, that's all. He'd swallow a tale like that.'

'Only not from you.'

'Why not from me?'

Gently simply shook his head. Julia Tallis moaned and laid her head on her husband's arm.

Between his teeth Raymond Tallis said: 'I wrote that letter. I wrote it there at Julia's bureau. I gave it to Fiona myself. When her memory comes back that's what she'll tell you.'

'Oh Ray ... no.'

He stroked her head. 'This is the way it's got to be.'

'Ray, I won't have it.'

To Gently, Raymond Tallis said: 'I'm ready to go now.'

'No – no!' Julia Tallis jumped up. 'He's telling you lies, and you shan't believe them. We know. We know who killed Freddy. It's for me he's telling all these lies.'

'Julia – shut up!'

'I won't, Ray – I'm not going to stand by and see you do it. I thought I could, but I can't.' She burst into a storm of tears. 'Listen to me – listen! What was Freddy wearing when he was killed? I'll tell you – I'll show you what he was wearing. The clothes are right here in the hall.'

'Julie, stop this –!'

But she'd grabbed Gently's arm and was dragging him towards the hall. There stood a carved chest, the lid of which she flung back.

'Look – look!'

She rummaged in the chest and pulled out a pair of waterproof trousers. Then a red sailing jacket, at the sight of which Eyke caught his breath.

'He was wearing these – all the members wear them. They're a special line stocked by the club. And look at this photograph – see, see? They're the same height, the same build. As far as anyone knew, Ray was going sailing, this is what they'd expect him to wear.' Tears almost stifled her. 'And the letter – the letter ... that was intended for him! Ray always had an eye for Ruth ... and if Fiona had brought him the letter ...' She was fighting to stay coherent. 'It was Freddy who turned up. The right clothes ... right figure ... Oh God, can't you see now? And we knew ... after Paul came here. Ray ...' She broke down in helpless sobbing.

Beside them, Raymond Tallis stood stony-eyed, mouth jammed in a tight line.

Gently said to Eyke: 'You can confirm the jacket?'

'Yes, sir,' Eyke said. 'I'd say it's identical.'

'Fetch Paul Tallis.'

Eyke went out. Raymond Tallis put his arm round the blubbering Julia.

Gently said: 'I could charge you with obstruction.'

'Do your worst,' Raymond Tallis said.

'If I don't, it's because of Mrs Tallis.'

Raymond Tallis kept his mouth shut.

They waited, it seemed, for a long time, with Julia Tallis sobbing continually. When Eyke returned he was breathing rather fast and he motioned Gently aside.

'Sir ... young Tallis has hopped it. He isn't in the cottage or the grounds.'

They exchanged stares.

'Which way would he go?'

'Don't reckon he'd come past the gate, sir.'

'Then the ferry ...'

Eyke nodded. 'And that's the town, sir. Where there are buses.'

'Put out a general call and send a couple of men over the ferry.'

Eyke ducked out again. Gently returned to the loving couple. Raymond Tallis stared over his wife's dishevelled hair, a glint of malice in his eyes.

'So he's given you the slip, has he?'

Gently said: 'You're coming with me.'

'I'm coming where?'

'To The Uplands. Mrs Tallis may stay here.'

Raymond Tallis's eyes narrowed. 'Oh no. I'm not going there.'

'You're coming,' Gently said, 'if I have to put you in handcuffs. And when we get there you will follow instructions.'

'But listen, young Quennell will be at my throat −'

'Make your mind up how you want it to be.'

Raymond Tallis made his mind up. In the car outside Eyke was just finishing a call on RT. Seeing Tallis, he reached for a pad, scribbled a note and passed it to Gently. It read:

'Ipswich. Car described parked at station about 15.15.'

Shrugging, Gently passed the pad back.

'So that's how he missed Brazil's goal.'

12

They ran the gauntlet, Tallis with his head ducked and his face concealed in his hands. At once the press cavalcade was on the move at their heels. At the cones cameramen hustled up and flashes fizzed at the car windows, but by now Tallis was lying flat, his hands clasped over his head. Finally they drove clear into the refuge of the private road.

'That was ... disgraceful! Why didn't you stop it?'

His face was white, his eyes stunned.

'We'll give them a proper statement later, sir,' Eyke said soothingly. 'Don't you worry about them.'

'But what good is that? Tomorrow morning I'll be on the front page of every cheap rag ...'

At The Uplands Reymerston was just leaving; he stared curiously at Tallis, who scowled back furiously. To Gently Reymerston said:

'Ruth is upstairs with Fiona. They've got her to take something and lie down.'

'She's not drugged?'

'Just a shot of brandy. But she's scarcely *compos mentis*. Grey has been and left a prescription. I'm going to get it made up.' He hesitated. 'What's on?'

'We want to lay hands on Paul Tallis.'

'Paul ...?'

'If you see him, get in touch with us at once.'

Reluctantly, Reymerston left. In the porch of The Uplands, Frank Quennell waited belligerently. He and Tallis eyed each other like a pair of bristling mastiffs.

'That man isn't coming in here.'

'Step aside, Mr Quennell.'

'No, I won't. His presence is an insult. I wonder he dare show his face.'

'Mr Tallis is here at my request.'

'He'll never come into this house again.'

'It was you who put him on to me,' Tallis snarled. 'You stupid young fool. Now look at all the trouble you've made.'

'I told him the truth –'

'A fairy-tale!'

'I tell you, you're not coming into the house ...'

Gently grabbed each by an arm. 'Listen, you two! When I like I can make myself very unpleasant. So you'll just shut up and do as I tell you, or maybe you'll both spend a night in the cells.'

'But you've no right to bring him here –'

'Get inside!'

Frank Quennell retreated and let them into the house.

The lounge was on the left; opposite, across the hall, was the door of Quennell's study. Gently ushered them into it: a room full of books with a roll-top desk occupying one corner.

'Now! You'll wait here, Mr Tallis, along with the Inspector. You're to keep quiet till I call for you, and then you're to come through into the lounge. Understood?'

Tallis nodded sullenly.

'Mr Quennell will fetch his mother and sister.'

'No, I won't –!'

Gently's hand fell on his arm: he propelled him outside and towards the stairs.

'I tell you she's asleep. The doctor –'

'Request their presence in the lounge.'

'But ... it's sheer cruelty!'

'You will not mention Mr Tallis.'

He gave Frank Quennell a helping shove to send him stumbling up the stairs. Then he half-closed the study door and crossed into the lounge. Voices sounded above: Frank Quennell's subdued bass and the enquiring murmur of Ruth Quennell. From the study, no sound. At last, footsteps on the stairs. Ruth Quennell entered first.

'I don't understand, Superintendent ...'

Behind her, Fiona Quennell hovered warily in the doorway. Her eyes looked dazed; she was gazing at Gently as though she couldn't properly make him out; yet she was ready for flight. Over her shoulder, Frank Quennell's face scowled anxiously.

'Please come in and sit down. Mr Quennell, leave the door ajar.'

'But I thought you'd finished with Oona,' Ruth Quennell said.

'Please! I don't think we should question her again.'

'This shouldn't take long. If you will be kind enough to sit with your daughter on the settee.'

'Oona's been asleep ...'

'A simple question. Only the answer is important.'

Ruth Quennell shook her head, but beckoned Fiona Quennell into the room. After a long pause, Fiona Quennell entered and crept across to the settee. Ruth Quennell sat with her; Frank Quennell remained by the door. Fiona Quennell's eyes still looked bemused; she was frowning as she gazed at Gently.

'Do I know this man, mummy?'

'Hush, darling! He has something to say to you.'

'I feel I ought to know him ... and yet –' She shuddered. 'Have I done something foolish lately?'

'Nothing, darling.'

'My mind is so funny. It's as though I'm still in a dream. But I think I know him.' She smiled suddenly at Gently. 'How do you do!'

'Hush, darling.'

'But I'm sure I know him.'

'Yes, dear.'

'He was here before.' The smile vanished and her mouth quivered. 'It's about daddy ... isn't it?'

'Yes, dear. About daddy.'

Fiona Quennell began to sob.

Gently said: 'Miss Quennell.'

She stared at him dazedly, through tears.

'Miss Quennell, when I was here before you told me what you did with a letter.'

'A letter ...'

'Yes, a letter. Somebody gave you a letter. You threw the letter away, but really you should have taken it somewhere.'

Her eyes were getting fierce behind the tears. 'Mummy knows all about that.'

'About what ...?'

'I'm never going to get married. But I shall write letters when I go away.'

'Somebody else gave you this letter.'

'Never – never. Do you hear?'

'You had to take the letter to someone.'

'I never will – I never will!'

'Mr Tallis!' Gently called.

Tallis's heavy step crossed the hall. Sulkily he came through the door, stood defiantly staring from one to other of them.

'Miss Quennell, isn't this the man to whom you were asked to take the letter?'

Fiona Quennell's eyes sprang wide open and she jerked up from the settee. Gurgling, making strange noises, saliva dribbling down her chin, she stood glaring at Raymond Tallis, her fingers hooking at air. Then she screamed piercingly, her eyes rolled and she collapsed.

'See to her!'

Frank Quennell rushed forward to help his mother pick her up. They got her on the settee, and Frank Quennell stuffed a cushion under her head. She lay trembling, eyes closed, breath coming in ragged snatches. Whimpering, Ruth Quennell found a handkerchief and wiped the saliva from her daughter's face.

'You'll pay for this – it's beyond everything!'

'If there are smelling salts, you'd better fetch them.'

'But you'll pay –!' Frank Quennell dashed away, and one heard his feet clamour on the stairs.

Gently said to Tallis: 'That's it. You can wait in the car.'

'But this ... this is terrible!'

'Do as I say.'

Looking stricken, Tallis shambled away.

'My sister is asking to talk to you.'

For twenty minutes, Gently had smoked his pipe in the study: not an uninteresting room, since Quennell had been something of a collector. Among books representing the history of printing Gently had found a couple of incunabula, both English, one an almanac printed by Wynkyn de Worde.

Eyke meanwhile had sat in the car, staying in touch with the RT. But as yet no word had come through of any sighting of Paul Tallis.

'Your sister is calm again?'

'No thanks to you.' Frank Quennell was maintaining his pose of outrage. 'If it rested with me, you could go to hell. But mother thinks you should come.'

Gently put away his pipe and followed Frank Quennell. Fiona

Quennell was sitting up and drinking something from a tumbler. Though pale she appeared to be quite collected, and her eyes had lost their fixed stare. Ruth Quennell sat with an arm round her daughter. She gave Gently a look of appeal; she took the tumbler. Fiona Quennell said in a low voice:

'You know ... don't you?'

'Yes, I know.'

Gently pulled up a chair. Fiona Quennell sat with downcast eyes for a while, then she asked:

'Have you ... found him?'

'We're looking for him.'

'Where is he?'

'A short time ago he was at the cottage. Then he went off towards the ferry.'

'I see.'

Her mouth trembled a little but she made it firm again.

'He's a child really.'

'I know.'

'You won't hurt him.'

'We won't hurt him.'

'It's me who's to blame. I told him something that he could never get out of his mind.'

'We know. about that.'

'No you don't. It was something I heard in the summerhouse. It was the day after Uncle Arthur ... daddy and Uncle Ray were in the garden, talking about it.'

'Do you wish to tell me?'

She nodded. 'It was about throwing the marker overboard. Uncle Ray was on deck several minutes before daddy, but he hadn't thrown in a marker or done anything at all. Perhaps he was in a panic. According to daddy, they'd probably searched in the wrong area. With the direction of the current they could have been half a mile out. I was horrified. I had dreams for weeks.' She looked down at her lap. 'And I told Paul.'

'He believed his uncle had done it deliberately.'

'Yes. Especially when they lied at the inquest. And he knew about Aunty Julie, of course ... that had never been a secret. Then it all piled up. They got married, and Uncle Ray made daddy managing director. Paul said it was proof. The way he talked frightened me ... especially just lately, during the vacation. At times he seemed very wild, talking about his father and about natural justice. But I didn't think it was serious. Paul is like that. He isn't really wicked, just so young.'

'Do you remember Saturday?'

She shuddered. 'He was in his wild state when he came in here. He'd got the letter. He was waving it about and calling it his instrument of justice. I asked him what it was, but he wouldn't tell me, told me I would know soon enough. He said I was to take it to Uncle Ray, but not to tell him who it came from. I said I wouldn't. He said yes, or he'd never speak to me again. He took me in his car to the top of the road, and waited to see me on my way to the Lodge.'

'Did you notice anything in the car?'

'Something under a rug in the back.'

'Did he refer to it?'

She shook her head. 'But it was too long to lie flat across the seat.'

'Which way did he drive off?'

'Up the street. I kept looking back till I saw he was gone.'

'What did you do then?'

'I came home again. I had no intention of delivering the letter. I didn't know what it was, but I guessed it must be something very unpleasant. I wanted to get rid of it. I went down the garden. I was going to tear it up and shove it into the composter. Only daddy was down there, he saw me with it, I had to come back to the house. And he followed me up. I slipped into the kitchen, and just had time to stick it in the swing-bin. Daddy asked me about it —' her lips twitched painfully '– and I told him it was the envelope off a circular.'

'Did he believe you?'

'I – I thought he did. He just went to the sink to wash his hands. And I went upstairs. And that's all ... until the policeman showed me the l-letter on Sunday ...'

Ruth Quennell's arm tightened around her, but Fiona Quennell shrugged it away. She reached for the tumbler and drank from it. There was moisture on her pale forehead.

'What's going to happen to him?'

'You'll be able to visit him.'

She shivered. 'Will it be very long?'

'Everything will be considered. There'll be certain tests. At a guess, he'll get a minimum sentence.'

'Tests ...?'

'The court will ask for them.'

In her eyes a trace of the stare had returned. 'Perhaps I should be there with him. I knew what he was thinking, but I didn't tell anyone.'

'You couldn't have known.'

'Yes ... he talked about it, about being his father's avenger. Only it was half a game, I didn't believe it, everything was half a game with Paul. You went along with him or he lost his temper. But it was always half a game.'

'You were fond of him.'

'I don't love him, you know. Just that I always feel terribly responsible.' Her head dropped over the tumbler. 'Shall I see him now?'

'Do you want to see him?'

'No.'

Outside a car pulled up noisily, making Fiona Quennell start. One heard voices, then a step in the hall and Eyke's face showed at the door.

'Sir ...'

Gently rose and went out. Reymerston waited in the porch. On the painter's face was a look of concern and he took Gently by the arm.

'Listen ... just now I called at my place and happened to look towards the harbour. There was a yacht under sail. I put glasses on it. It was Quennell's Dragon, and the helmsman was Paul Tallis.'

'Paul Tallis! Are you certain?'

'More than certain. I jumped in my car and drove down there. I ran along the jetty, calling to him, telling him he was wanted and that weather was blowing up. He must have heard me, but he wouldn't turn his head, just kept jilling along down the harbour. If he's going out, he'll be in trouble. A Dragon is a bitch to single-handle.'

'The bloody young fool.'

'Perhaps he'll listen to you ...'

But Gently was already running to the car. Eyke jumped in beside him; the engine fired, and the Princess scoured away in a rattle of chippings.

'What – what –?'

They'd forgotten Raymond Tallis, who sat gaping in the seat behind.

Already the breeze was bending the heads of the poplars that grew along the private road.

If anything the press cavalcade had grown and now was towing behind them like a royal entourage. The crowd, which had begun to stray after the departure of Tallis, came back running at the sight of the cars. Above the piles of the jetty a sail was still bobbing, held back by the flood and the jetty's obstruction. Gently swerved the Princess into the visitors' park and drove on to the boundary posts. He and Eyke piled out.

'You too, Mr Tallis!'

'But why – what –?'

'I may need the advice of a yachtsman.'

Tallis, press and all, they plugged over the salt-marsh and up on to the rugged framework of the jetty. The Dragon had fifty yards to go before it cleared the harbour mouth: it was inching along over the tide, driven only by puffs in the top of the sail. Paul Tallis sat low at the helm, face turned up to the shifting pennant. The jib, which he'd cleated, flapped unhappily, catching only eddies and down-draughts. Gently came to a stand above the yacht.

'Put about, Mr Paul!'

Cameramen ran to kneel on the rough timbers, others manoeuvred to catch Gently in the foreground. But Paul Tallis ignored them all. His solemn face continued turned towards the pennant. Under his arm nestled the tiller, in his hand the soft propylene sheet.

'Mr Paul, there's weather coming up. It isn't safe for you to go out.'

Not a flicker showed in his face, and his only movement was the nursing of the tiller.

'Can you hear what I say?'

No response. It was as though he were acting out some scene. Up on the jetty they were merely an audience, to be ignored by the man holding centre stage. Reporters, cameramen ran ahead: every moment cameras clicked at the blue-hulled Dragon.

'You're running into danger – don't you understand?'

If he did, it meant nothing to him.

'We shall have to send out a lifeboat to rescue you.'

Perhaps, secretly, that was what he was wanting!

Ignored by the reporters, Tallis stood scowling at the blue boat. Suddenly you realised that those creased, narrowed eyes were the eyes of a yachtsman, a seafarer. He was measuring the distance between yacht and jetty. But it was too far for the most desperate of leaps.

'Paul – it's me! Pull over a bit.'

'No heroics,' Gently muttered.

'If he goes out there alone he's a goner. There's a gale brewing out of this.'

'He's acting a part.'

'Then it'll bloody drown him, and lose a boat worth more than he is.'

'Keep it down.'

'Paul!' Raymond Tallis shouted. 'You need cruising rig, boy, if you're going out there.'

Paul Tallis sailed on. By yard and yard, he was beating the flood to the jetty's end. An extra puff over their heads brought up the boot-topping and hastened him on. And when he cleared the jetty, wind enough then, with a dangerous broad reach to rush him seawards ... did he mean to do it? With his audience growing by the moment, the odds were that he'd shrink from an anticlimax ...

'Get his mother out here.'

'What –? You're mad!'

'If she can't talk him in, nobody will.'

'The reporters – the cameramen –'

'It's her son! On your way and get her out here.'

Raymond Tallis gaped for a moment, then scuttled away towards the house. But the chances of her getting there in time were remote: the Dragon had only twenty yards to make.

'Sir, I could turn out the inshore lifeboat,' Eyke murmured in his ear.

'How long do you reckon it would take to get here?'

'Well, sir, if the crew were handy ...'

'We'll hold them back till we see what he does.'

He shifted on down the jetty, which here had awkward gaps below which water swirled. A cameraman, bolder than the rest, was climbing out on the baulks at the very end. And now the reporters were trying their hand:

'Sonny, pull in and let us aboard!'

'It could be worth a packet ...'

'If you need a lawyer, my paper ...'

'Shut up!' Gently snarled at them.

'Chiefie, we've got a right –'

But they did shut up, murmuring amongst themselves and scrambling on a bit further along the piles. And Paul Tallis had taken not a scrap of notice. You might have thought he was in a different world.

'Mr Paul, you've had your fun, and you'll be in danger if you take it further ... can you hear me?'

The jib had picked up: at its seaward end the jetty consisted only of skeleton piles.

'Listen ... your mother's on her way. She's expecting you to be here to talk to her. Put your turn in now, before you pick up too much wind ...'

But slowly the Dragon was increasing speed, ready to launch into the chop outside.

Then, from up the jetty, came a cry: 'Cooee, Paul – cooee!'

It wasn't Julia Tallis but Fiona Quennell who came stumbling and jumping over the timbers. Behind her was Reymerston and her brother, with Ruth Quennell some distance back. Fiona Quennell's black hair was flying and she sprang panting on to the baulk beside Gently.

'Paul, you idiot – it's Oona!'

Paul Tallis half turned his head.

'Listen, you nitwit. Stop acting the goat, and bring daddy's boat back at once!'

Now he turned to look full up at her. Fiona Quennell made an imperious gesture.

'Come on, chump ... put about! You know you'll have to in a minute ...'

But that was when the wind hit him. First, the jib cracked and bellied full. At once the Dragon heeled and began to rush forward out of the shelter of the jetty. It plunged in the chop, the mainsail filled and suddenly the yacht was on its ear. All its red bottom heaved out of the water and stayed for a moment, gleaming.

'Oh ... he'll drown!'

But the Dragon heaved up again, wet sails empty and flogging. They could see Paul Tallis again, working furiously to free the jib-sheet. The yacht pitched and bounded, hanging in the wind; then the jib was trimmed and she bore away. Finally, he got a trim on the mainsail, when, heeling firmly, she began to travel.

'But he'll never get her in again ... he can't!'

Yet the crisis seemed over, just for that moment. Clearly Paul Tallis had regained control, and the wind, though puffy, was not yet strong. On a sensible course, with wind abeam, he appeared to be out of immediate danger.

'Call out the inshore boat.'

Eyke hurried away to take care of it. The reporters, their dash of excitement over, now wanted to turn their attention to Gently.

'Chiefie, we know Paul Tallis is chummie ...'

'Just hold your horses for a statement!'

A better look-out was to be had from the sand dunes, and, shouldering through the reporters, he set off there. Everyone else moved off too – the jetty had been a comfortless perch! Fiona Quennell was sticking close to her brother; the flash of spirit had gone out of her. Reymerston chaperoned Ruth Quennell. Across the car park, too late, Raymond Tallis hastened with his wife.

'Is he all right?'

'He made it outside.'

'Oh lord,' Julia Tallis said. 'Not him as well.'

'The inshore boat will pick him up.'

'It's exactly a year since Arthur ...'

Fiona Quennell ran to Julia Tallis: 'Oh, Aunty Jule ... oh, I'm so sorry!'

Tearfully, Julia Tallis hugged her. 'It'll be all right.'

'Oh I'm so sorry – for everyone!'

They scrambled up the sand dunes. All along the tops people were crowding for vantage points. The yacht now was quarter of a mile offshore and sliding bravely over the waves. Every so often her sail fluttered, indicating that Paul Tallis was sailing her loose. Nevertheless she was slipping along fast, holding a course due south-east. Eyke rejoined them.

'The boat's on its way, sir. Should be along in a few minutes.'

'Have you sent a man with her?'

'DC Bayliss. They'll be off when they've picked him up.'

'Where will they bring him?'

'To the ferry landing. I've put some uniform men down there.'

'I want it sealed off.'

'Yes, sir. Those were the instructions I gave them.'

Raymond Tallis said: 'If this weather holds off, that young devil could fetch Holland.'

Julia Tallis watched with haunted eyes, her handsome face tear-ravaged.

An engine moaned up river, then buzzed, mosquito-like, towards the jetty. One could hear it grumble and snarl as it met the chop outside the harbour. Into view bounced the orange inflatable, its three crouched crew bulky in life-jackets; slamming and moaning, it set off over the waves in the track of the Dragon. It was doubling her speed, or more: a marine terrier hot on the trail. The Dragon continued her sliding pace, aristocratically unmoved by the ruffian astern.

Julia Tallis gasped: 'Oh ... they won't hurt him!'

'It'll be his own fault if they do,' Raymond Tallis said. 'But they know what they're up to.'

After watching for a moment, Reymerston ran back to his car, to return with glasses.

Steadily the gap lessened; yet it took longer to close than at first seemed probable. The further the two craft moved away, the less was the apparent differential in speed. Finally the lifeboat appeared to be dogging the yacht and making no ground at all. Then suddenly the yacht bobbed visibly, its sails yawing about.

'What's happening ...?'

'I can't quite see ... he's shoved her up into the wind.'

Gently took the glasses from Reymerston and trained them on the boats. The blue hull was now visible, now concealed as it bobbed between crest and trough; the orange lifeboat, instead of closing with her, was bobbing too, at a short distance. It moved on a little, bobbed again, and at long last spurted to join the yacht. A man scrambled into her. There was some confusion with flogging sails and a bouncing boom.

'Well ... they've got her!'

First the main, then the jib were pulled down from the wagging mast. But the two boats continued to bob there, riding uneasily side by side. What was going on? Gently caught a glimpse of a man in the act of throwing something overside: something that glinted colour for an instant then was lost in the waves. What ...? Minutes dragged by before the boats began to move. Then it was slowly, very slowly, the lifeboat lashed alongside the yacht.

149

Raymond Tallis said surlily: 'Let me have the glasses!'

He squinted through them for a long time; then, coming close to Gently, he muttered:

'He isn't with them ...'

Gently grabbed the glasses back. Three figures were visible, one in the yacht, two in the lifeboat. Each wore a life-jacket. Unless he lay prone, Paul Tallis was not on the boats.

'He could be under the shelter ...'

'He's gone. I saw them throw in a marker.'

Gently stared into the squinting eyes. 'Get your wife back to the house.'

As though instinctively she knew what had passed, Julia Tallis set up a wail.

'I want to stay here – I want to see him!'

But Tallis was forcibly pulling her away. He dragged her, weeping and imploring, down the sand dunes, his arm implacable round her waist.

Gently said to Reymerston: 'You too. Take Mrs Quennell and her daughter.'

'No, I'm staying, I'm staying!' Fiona Quennell cried.

'Go with your mother. Mrs Tallis needs you.'

'Oh Paul, poor Paul!' Fiona Quennell cried.

Reymerston grabbed both their arms.

The tandem tow came in very slowly, the yacht dragging at the lifeboat with its slower pitch. Now there was a rush back to the jetty, with the reporters and cameramen in the van. Gently let them go. He nodded to Eyke, and together they went down towards the ferry. There the minibus stood blocking the approach and six uniformed men waited. Nobody spoke. Some fishermen had appeared from the huts and stood watching. It must have been twenty minutes later when lifeboat and yacht edged in to the staging. Gently went out to it.

'Well?'

The crewman cut his engine.

'The young bugger jumped. I saw him stuff something into his pocket ... ballast.'

'You couldn't get to him.'

'He went down like a stone. We were fifty yards away. I've buoyed the spot with a net-float, but there's a funny old current out there.'

'How deep?'

'Seven or eight fathom.'

'Put the yacht back on moorings and give the officer your statement.'

And that was all. Perhaps he'd have done it in the harbour if they'd gone after him sooner; or perhaps he wouldn't.

A Greek tragedy ...?

The chorus, the press, were clamouring for a hand-out.

13

Somehow, Gently had kept the secret for forty-eight hours, from Thursday till Saturday; but only because Gabrielle's attention had been focused on the flat. He had taken time off to meet her at Heathrow when, after the first fine flush of greeting, she had placed her finger on his chin and said:

'My friend, I have many ideas ...'

Apparently she had rung the decorators before she left, and on Friday all chaos broke out at Lime Walk; they had spent the evening among stripped walls, the stench of paint and dust-sheeted furniture. And all day she'd been dashing round the shops choosing furniture, carpets, curtains. Then, tired but triumphant, she'd produced a splendid savoury omelette, followed by a gâteau, Roquefort and *petits fours*.

'Something simple. I will do better another time.'

They had eaten it in the kitchen among paint-cans and wallpaper. And it was only then, when they sat with their coffee, that she had asked:

'Who is this Mrs Jonson who invites us to stay?'

Because that had been his story, an invitation, accepted to get them away from the muddle of the flat. Gabrielle had barely given it a thought until this precise moment.

'I met her when I was out there this week. She's the wife of an American Airforce Colonel.'

'Aha. And I am not to be jealous?'

'Why not? She's an attractive woman.'

'She will not cook as well as I, my friend. These American women I know.'

'Actually she's English.'

'Then the matter is settled. She either cooks badly or very badly.'

'She makes good lemonade.'

'Her hair will be dyed. I cannot be jealous of such a person.'

'You'll love the place.'

And he had almost told her then, suddenly seeing her in that setting. Instead he had praised the country, the coast, the village and the heather that rolled to Mrs Jonson's door.

The heather ...!

Just a small anxiety was that it would be past its best by Saturday; but no. When they met it, beyond Ipswich, the heather was still pulsating with electric blueness. The day too was perfect: sun after mist, hazy, the air scented with autumn. Here and there a yellow leaf was showing and bracken paling to fawn. And Gabrielle beside him was drinking it in.

'This is country of great charm, my friend. It has style. It is now and then like Normandy. Would not this be a good place to seek for a home?'

'You would like that?'

'Yes, I think. Do you not tell me there are good beaches?'

'At a village near here there is a vineyard.'

'Aha. But the wine will be like vinegar.'

So they came to the village, and the road through the gorse, and the rusty wall, the gates, the house. And there once more children played on the lawn while, further down, someone was painting at an easel. It was Reymerston; looking rather absurd in a decorator's apron, its pocket sagging with brushes. But Gabrielle was gazing at the house.

'This place, my friend ... what did you call it?'

'Heatherings. Just the other side of that hedge are acres and acres of heather.'

'Ah yes, I smell it. Lucky Mrs Jonson.'

'Unfortunately she has to leave it. Her husband has been posted to Washington, and she must follow him very soon.'

'To leave this house? The poor lady. I would not leave it for a dozen Washingtons.'

'Her husband was sad too. But a serviceman goes where he is sent.'

Then Sarah Jonson came hurrying out: 'Oh, you've arrived ... please introduce me!' She seized Gabrielle's hand eagerly, eating her up with a fascinated gaze.

'So you're the famous Gabrielle – of course, I was wild to have you down here.'

'Madame ...?'

'I want to ask you so much, all about what happened up there in

Scotland. My goodness, you were brave. I talked to Larry on the phone, and he was just sick at having missed you.'

'Madame Sarah, I am admiring your house.'

'Oh, that. Come in, and I'll show you all over.'

She swept Gabrielle into the house, and Gently followed with their bags. Now he had actually got a foot in there, was dumping his belongings in one of the rooms. And Gabrielle, had she begun to guess? She was only half-listening to Sarah Jonson's prattle. Like a picture in a frame was her bold figure in the benevolent rooms, on the spacious stairway ...

'Is it that I may see the kitchen?'

'This way. Larry had the fitments shipped over.'

'It is not now long before you join your husband ...?'

'At first I hated the idea. Now, I want to get away.'

Diplomatically, Gently drifted off out of the house and down the lawn. Reymerston threw him a grin but, for the moment, continued his brushwork. He was painting the house. In his troubling style he was evoking the subject in that autumn moment, the rounded gables in hazy sky, the children, flowers and sunny lawn. It was nearly done. He seemed to work recklessly, throwing paint at passages that appeared quite perfect. Then they became something else, troubling, challenging you with new comment. Gently lit his pipe and watched. Finally Reymerston stood away.

'That's it, I think.'

'How do you know?'

'Something clicks and you have to finish.'

'Who is it for?'

'Sarah. She wanted one to take away.'

He squeezed a brush in an oily rag, then sat on the grass beside his easel. Gently sat too. The two women appeared at an upper window: Gabrielle waved.

'And that's her?'

Gently nodded.

'You're a lucky devil,' Reymerston said. 'Ruth, she's carted Fiona off to Oban, to relatives there. She thought it best. The Tallises have cleared off too. You've damned near depopulated Walderness.'

Gently said: 'Did you tell Ruth?'

Reymerston plucked a daisy. 'Yes.'

'So.'

'She asked if you knew about it and I told her that you did. She said but he's still your friend, and I said yes, I thought you still were, and she said so he doesn't blame you, and I said yes, perhaps.' He flipped the daisy. 'Then she said Andy, if he can trust you, I can.' He slid a glance at Gently. 'You can tell her you don't, but I doubt if it will make very much difference. I asked her to marry me. She said yes. And that's the state of play, old lad.'

'When is the wedding?'

'Oh, some time next year. Are you buying the house, by the way?'

'Perhaps.'

'Do I rate an introduction to Madame?'

'First take off that ridiculous apron.'

Reymerston sighed and stretched out on the grass. 'They haven't found him, you know,' he said. 'A couple of days they had divers out there. I can't look at that sea and feel the same. I went to the inquest on Quennell. Tallis was there, but not his missus. Under sedation, they tell me. She wasn't at the second inquest, either. What a bloody mess.' He sighed again, staring up at the soft sky. 'I'll tell you the last belief of a noble mind. It is that somewhere there's a moral purpose.'

Gently said: 'I've met a man, Edwin Keynes, who wasn't content to leave it so indefinite.'

'What was his idea?'

'It turned on a metaphysic. He was looking for a fundamental error in philosophy.'

'And did he find it?'

'To his own satisfaction. He says it lies in our concept of time, space and being. According to Keynes these are arbitrary concepts which we derive from aspects of motion.'

'Do we?' Reymerston said, turning on his elbow. 'But this is going back to Heraclitus.'

'Only,' Gently said, 'in Keynes' case, he has the backing of modern physics. Matter breaks down into patterns of energy or, as Keynes would have it, motion. Time is a domestic measure for speeds of motion. Space, a description of motional relations.'

'This is getting ingenious,' Reymerston said. 'But if all is motion, what is it that moves?'

'Keynes simply points to the results of research,' Gently said.

'Nothing solid has ever been discovered in matter. To quote him, simple or atomic motion expresses itself without an object.'

Reymerston was beginning to smile. 'That's cheeky. I would like to spend an hour with this fellow. But I don't see how it bears on the question of moral purpose.'

'It connects like this. According to Keynes, no distinction is possible between mental and physical motion. It follows that there can be no valid distinction between a concept and a phenomenon. An example in one aspect may find identity with an example in the other.'

'Oh glory,' Reymerston laughed. 'And he finds an identity for moral purpose?'

'Well, the ethical principle,' Gently said. 'Which he defines as a direction from hate to love. He regards this as the most primitive moral principle, requiring the most primitive physical principle to equate with. The phenomenon he selects is the dispersal of energy, which involves direction from potential to equilibrium. So he obtains a motional reality essentially ethical in character.'

'And you go along with that?' Reymerston laughed.

Gently blew a smoke-ring. 'Wouldn't you?'

'It's a charming idea,' Reymerston smiled. 'But I would need to go over the logic again. I seem to remember Sartre shaping up to this one, and then quietly backing away.'

'Perhaps Sartre was still stuck with time, space and being.'

'Perhaps,' Reymerston smiled. 'Or perhaps he didn't walk the beach by moonlight.'

'Edwin Keynes is a lover of trees.'

The two women came out of the house and Reymerston jumped up and pulled off his apron. He offered a hastily-scrubbed hand to Gabrielle, who went at once to stare at the picture.

'I will buy, monsieur.'

Reymerston grinned. 'The house is for sale, but not the picture.'

'Monsieur has a talent that is unique.'

'I believe Monsieur George is of a similar opinion.'

'I too wish a picture of this house.'

'He never paints them twice,' Sarah Jonson said.

Gently said: 'I'll show Gabrielle the heather.'

He took her arm and led her down to the gate. If anything, the heather was more blue than it had been at the beginning of the week. Haze smudged the distant trees and the slender spire of the church, bees buzzed drunkenly, the broad bosom of the heath exhaled scent in warm waves. She clung to his arm in delight, taking deep breaths of the heady odour.

'Did you like the house?'

'Oh, my dear!'

'Shall we not live there?'

He felt her arm tighten.

'I think it is possible. There are trains to town. I shall of course sell my house in Finchley.'

She stared up at him, her eyes in a dazzle.

'I could be – mistress, of that house there?'

'Mistress of Heatherings.'

'I dare not believe it!'

'Sarah is holding the sale for us.'

She hid her face against him, very still, scarcely breathing. But when she looked up at him again her face was wet with tears.

'I am a fool – I cannot help it! You should not have told me this so suddenly. I wanted ... I wished ... I did not know! All at once, my life has become as a dream. And this is possible?'

'It's a long way from Heathrow ...'

'Oh, you idiot of a man. I have secrets too that I do not tell. What do you think I am doing in Rouen?'

'In Rouen ...?'

'Yes – yes. I do not go just to order stock. I have taken Andrée into a notary's, and soon now she is a full partner. Do you not see? Perhaps once a month is all I need now to be in France. How can I part from you more often? Am I a woman made of stone?'

'You have done this –?'

'I tell you yes. I am your wife now every day. And together we shall buy this house – in all things, everything, together! Oh my friend, why do I cry? In my heart there is too much joy.'

She burrowed her face in his jacket, to cry again without sobs. But almost at once she pulled away to stare at him with anxious eyes.

'She is holding the sale? Oh, let us close it!'

'But we can do nothing on a Saturday.'

'Ah yes – come – we must clap hands. My friend, I am business, you are not.'

She fairly tugged him back through the gate. Sarah Jonson and Reymerston were still appraising the painting. The children had joined them: they formed a small group at the corner of the lawn. Gently held Gabrielle's arm:

'Just a moment.'

Noon sun was flush on the bricks of the house, on the twin gables, the casement windows, the four dormers, the graceful porch. Shining where it had shone for most of three centuries, while martins had trained their flights to the eaves, while the scent of heather had stolen into the rooms: under such chalky Suffolk skies ...

'Oh, my friend – come along!'

Reluctantly Gently followed her.

'Monsieur,' she said to Reymerston, 'I have changed my mind. I no longer wish the picture – I will take the house!'

Brundall, 1980–81

NOTE

I wish to acknowledge a hint for the above book taken from a Warwickshire author, a man who went to London and made a few bob writing before returning to his native county. He too had literary debts.

A.H.

158